*Dedicated to the Galápagos Islands,
one of the world's last wild places,
where animals roam free and humans
are strictly controlled.*

For further information, contact:
Tumblehome, Inc.
201 Newbury St, Suite 201
Boston, MA 02116
http://tumblehomebooks.org/

Library of Congress Control Number 2019940378
ISBN-13 978-1-943431-55-7
ISBN-10 1-943431-55-8

Prager, Ellen
Escape Galápagos / Ellen Prager - 1st ed
Illustrated by Melissa Logies

Printed in Taiwan

10 9 8 7 6 5 4 3 2 1

TUMBLEHOME, Inc.

Escape Galápagos

Book One of
The Wonder List Adventures

Ellen Prager

Illustrated by Melissa Logies

GALAPAGOS ISLANDS
ECUADOR

Pinta

Santiago

Rabida

Pinzon

Fernandina

Isabela

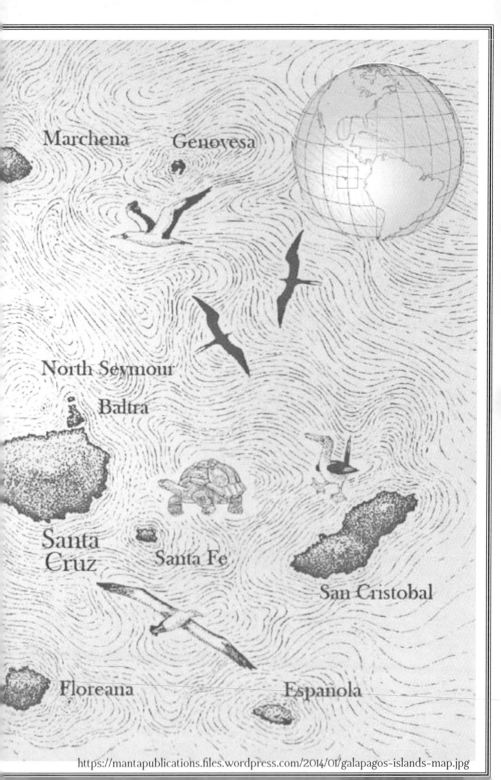

Marchena

Genovesa

North Seymour

Baltra

Santa Cruz

Santa Fe

San Cristobal

Floreana

Española

When Ezzy Skylar's mother died, her father swore to honor his wife's life of adventure by bringing the family to all of her must-see places—it was what she called her wonder list. Number one on that list was the Galápagos Islands. Twelve-year-old Ezzy had no idea that their very first trip would be the scariest, most exciting week of her life, and put all of their lives in danger.

Godzilla Sneezes

She lay low behind the castle. The darkly primeval creature appeared huge. Its skin was thick, black, and leathery. But what really worried Ezzy were its long, sharp claws. The beast crawled toward her. She ducked lower and inched backward. The animal stopped and sniffed the air. Ezzy stayed as still as possible, holding her breath and praying it couldn't smell her. The crest of spines on the creature's black head now loomed over the castle's twin towers. It lumbered forward and broke through an outer wall. Ezzy trembled. She scooted further back. It was going to be a monster movie style annihilation for the place she was hiding behind.

"This place is toast," she muttered.

"Ezzy, look out!" her father shouted.

Ezzy had been testing her nerve with the creepy-looking creature. Now, she stood up and towered over the two-foot-long black iguana. She turned to her father. "Yeah dad, lucky Godzilla here isn't any bigger."

The iguana continued to crawl over and through the sand castle someone had built on the beach before they arrived. Then, in the midst of destroying the castle's sandy turrets and walls, it stopped abruptly and froze. The iguana sneezed—and gooey lizard snot went flying.

"Yuck!" Ezzy yelped, jumping out of the line of fire.

Luke, her younger brother, giggled. "Remember what the book said, Sis. That's how they get rid of salt. They sneeze. It's from the algæ they eat."

"Yeah, yeah. It's the only marine iguana in the world and it dives into the ocean to feed on algæ. But salty iguana goobers are not something I need to experience up close and personal. It's bad enough I'm staring at the thing. I'm going to have giant iguana nightmares tonight for sure."

Luke knelt down to get a closer look at the strange-looking reptile. "C'mon, Sis. It's cool. Looks like a miniature dinosaur."

"Yeah, you're so weird, you probably want it for a pet."

Luke ignored the "weird" comment and turned to his dad eagerly.

"Don't even think about it, son. Animals like this are

meant to be in the wild with others of their kind."

They were on a small, uninhabited island with a long sandy beach stretching along the coast. A few other marine iguanas lounged on the sand, together with some sleeping sea lions. Small birds flitted about the shrubs at the back of the beach.

Ezzy's father stepped closer to the iguana and squatted down to peer into its small black eyes. The staring match didn't last long. The iguana remained perfectly still while the lean, long-legged man shifted uncomfortably and nearly toppled over. He brushed a few wayward strands of brown hair from his face, stood up, and tipped his floppy broad-rimmed khaki hat to the creature. "Beauty lies in the eyes of the beast."

His two kids stared at him dubiously.

"Are you sure that's how it goes?" Luke asked.

"I think it's beauty lies in the eyes of the *beholder*, dad, not *beast*," Ezzy told him. She chuckled. Her father loved using old sayings. But he almost always got them wrong. Ezzy and her brother took great pleasure in pointing out his mistakes. It had become sort of a Skylar family game.

"Maybe," her father said winking. "But anyway, this is just the beginning of the true wonders we'll see here in the Galápagos."

Ezzy tried to look excited. She wanted to be excited. It was their first full day in the Galápagos Islands. They had flown in the previous afternoon, taken a rickety bus to a dock and then climbed into a zodiac (a big blow-up boat with an outboard engine). They had then motored out to their ship—the *Darwin Voyager.* With five decks, it was the biggest ship Ezzy had ever been on. The lower part of the hull was dark blue, while the superstructure above was white. Ezzy didn't think it was an exceptionally fancy or particularly large ship, but it seemed pretty seaworthy. *Then again,* she had thought, *look what they said about the Titanic.* For a week, they would be living on the *Darwin Voyager,* cruising around the Galápagos Islands to go hiking and snorkeling.

Before Ezzy's mother got sick, she made a list of all the wondrous places in the world she wanted to go. The Galápagos Islands were number one on the list. Evelyn Skylar was a famous marine geologist and super adventurous. She especially loved what she called science surprises—the unpredictability of nature.

More than anything, Ezzy wanted to be like her mother: adventurous, brave, and appreciative of the unexpected. But Ezzy didn't like surprises, and wild animals creeped her out and made her nervous. Unlike her little brother, who loved all living things—even creepy crawly bugs and snakes. It wasn't that Ezzy hated animals or anything. Cats and dogs were fine. But creatures out in nature, especially those with claws or big teeth—they were unpredictable and dangerous. Ezzy sometimes wondered why wild animals made her so nervous. Maybe she'd had a bad animal incident as a baby or something. Her mother used to hold her hand and try to coax her closer to squirrels and birds out in their backyard and take her to the zoo. Now, with her mother gone, Ezzy wasn't sure she'd ever get over the whole wild animals thing.

But Ezzy knew the trip to the Galápagos was important to her father, and Luke was going to love it. He needed cheering up; he'd been so sad and quiet ever since their mom died. Ezzy had sworn to make the most of being there and to somehow learn to deal with her weird fear of wild animals for their sake.

Looking around at the others on the beach from the ship, Ezzy realized everyone else was now oohing and aahing over two small dark brown sea lion pups that had just popped out of the water. The pups had big round eyes and little snouts with long whiskers. They were waddling playfully around on the floury white sand. Luke was mesmerized by the baby sea lions and they seemed to be drawn to him, scurrying his way.

"Son, remember the rules," his father said. "We have to stay eight feet away from the animals."

Luke turned to Ezzy. "See, Sis, how can you not like them. They're so cute."

Ezzy stared at her short, ten-year-old, slightly pudgy, freckle-faced brother. The adoring look on his face was almost enough to make her join the sea lion fan club. Then again, she had done some reading before coming to the Galápagos. She had discovered that sea lions have big sharp teeth and if they bite you, the wound can become infected—all red and oozing. There were photos. *Those things might look cute,*

Ezzy thought, *but in reality, they're dangerous wad-dling mega germ vessels with teeth.* She tried to look calm, but inside, yup, she was freaking out.

"They want to play," Luke said to his father.

"They can play with each other."

Ezzy was about to make a wisecrack about how her brother had the brains of a sea lion or something along those lines, when a much larger sea lion slid out of the water onto the beach. It was thickly muscular, nearly six feet long, had an enlarged hump on its fore-head, and began barking threateningly at the people on the beach.

Jorge, the stocky Galápagos Park Naturalist ac-companying the group, stepped forward. "Let's give this guy some room. He's the alpha male here, the beach master. A bull and very territorial."

Ezzy began to inch backward. She looked down so as not to trip and stopped abruptly. Her foot hovered over what Jorge called sea lion surprise—a big pile of white sea lion poop. She stepped carefully over it. The stuff smelled terrible, worse than the bathrooms at school. It wasn't just the wild animals Ezzy was worried about; it was also their poop. It was every-where.

The big sea lion paused as if deciding what to do.

"C'mon, Luke," Ezzy called.

The boy hadn't moved. He stood perfectly still and stared at the humongous sea lion. It seemed to be staring back at him with curiosity or wary caution. It reminded Ezzy of the time a stray dog bit her brother and he said it was just a misunderstanding. After what seemed like a last look at the boy, the bull sea lion turned and slid into the water, quickly disappearing from sight.

"Okay, everyone," Jorge announced. "If you'd like to go back to the ship let me know, otherwise we've got about an hour here for swimming and snorkeling."

Ezzy raised her hand. "Uh, excuse me. What about that big sea lion? He's in the water, right?"

"No worries there, Miss. He won't bother you as long as you don't bother him."

Ezzy's father and brother began putting on their snorkeling gear. "C'mon, Ez," said her dad. "The water looks great."

"I think I'll just hang out here on the beach and watch you guys."

Ezzy stared at the water. She liked to swim—in a pool—not in the ocean with a giant territorial sea lion and other unpredictable wild creatures. Besides, she'd looked it up on the Internet. There are sharks in the Galápagos.

Luke was all smiles. "C'mon Sis. It's gonna be awesome."

"You know there are sharks in there?"

"It's perfectly safe," her father assured her. "Look, most of the group is already in the water."

Glancing around, Ezzy realized he was right. Of the ten people in the group from the ship, all but one woman was in the water. Even the elderly couple that Ezzy didn't think would make it off the ship were in the water, along with the selfie twins. They were two older teenage girls traveling with their parents and a brother. They took photos non-stop and always had to be in the picture. Ezzy wondered if they had a waterproof case for their phones so they could take underwater selfies.

"Can you swim or are you *afraid?*" asked a dark-haired athletic-looking boy standing in waist deep water. He was the brother of the selfie twins and looked about Ezzy's age.

"What?" Ezzy snapped. "Of course I can swim."

"Looks like you're a little fraidy-cat girl to me," the boy teased. "Buck, buck, buck..."

Ezzy stared dumbfounded at the guy. He didn't even know her.

"It's probably too cold, or maybe you don't want to mess up your hair," the boy added laughing.

Ezzy gave the guy her best evil stare down and stomped over to the mesh bag containing her snorkeling gear. She didn't like that she was scared of wild animals, including those in the water, but she *really* hated it when people made fun of her, especially when they called her chicken. It made the fact that she wasn't as brave or as strong as her mother even worse. She grabbed her fins, mask, and snorkel, glared again at the boy, and jogged down to the water's edge. Her father gave her an encouraging thumbs up. Luke was already floating at his side.

Willing herself not to think about what kind of biting, clawing or slimy creatures were lurking in the water, Ezzy strode out to her father. The water was about two-feet deep, clear and calm.

"I can do this," she whispered to herself. "Think about what mom would do." Ezzy knew exactly what her mother would have done. She would have dived in and splashed around joyfully and then come back, grabbed her hand and gently talked her daughter into the water. A wave of sadness washed over Ezzy, but she knew it wasn't the time or place to be all gloomy about her mother's death or missing her. This trip was supposed to celebrate so many of the things her mother loved. Ezzy steeled herself and looked down.

White sand covered the bottom and, so far, she didn't see anything swimming around looking to take a bite out of her now slightly salted wet flesh.

"Here, let me help you," her father said, holding out a hand to steady her so she could put on her fins. *Don't freak out, don't freak out,* she thought. Then Ezzy looked up and saw that guy, she thought his name was Aiden. He was watching her with an annoying smirk on his face.

Luke started shouting excitedly. Through his snorkel, it was virtually impossible to decipher what he was yelling about. Ezzy thought he sounded like either a bizarre cow or really bad trumpet player. She glanced over at Aiden to see if he was still watching and then looked back at Luke. Her brother was pointing to something underwater, still jabbering through his snorkel.

Ezzy put on her mask and snorkel, getting ready to dive in. She hesitated and thought about what else could be in the water. She just couldn't do it. Instead, Ezzy leaned over and put her head underwater just enough to see what Luke was yelling about.

Her brother was nearby and still pointing to the bottom. A flat disc-shaped creature was swimming by. It was dark gray on top and white underneath, with wing-like fins and a short whip-like tail. Stingray. Ezzy stood up and backed away, thinking: *I'm no dummy, that's what killed that famous Australian animal guy.*

Her father also stood up and spit out his snorkel. "Ezzy, where are you going? It's just a stingray. They're harmless as long as you don't step on or harass them."

"Yeah, that's what they say about all dangerous and deadly creatures. They're fine until they kill you."

Her dad rolled his eyes and laughed. "Oh Ez, you've got to relax. Most animals are not going to hurt you." Then, looking a little sad, he added, "Your mom loved snorkeling, she would have dived right in."

"I know dad. I'm trying. Really."

He nodded and smiled warmly. "C'mon, let's see what other very nice and perfectly harmless creatures we can find."

It took a while, but eventually Ezzy was floating nervously beside her father and behind her brother. Luke was like the energizer bunny in the water, swimming back and forth and pointing to everything he saw.

"Look at that fish," Luke shouted, spitting out his snorkel. "Oooh, that one over there is really big and blue. There's a sea star and there's a sea turtle."

Ezzy kicked gently with her fins and cautiously floated closer to Luke. She looked down. On the bottom was a sea turtle about the size of a small coffee table. It had a big shield-shaped brown shell, speckled yellowish flippers, and a small rounded head. The sea turtle was munching on algæ and had some green stringy stuff hanging from its mouth. Ezzy decided it needed an undersea napkin. It was one of the least creepy animals she'd seen so far.

"Shark!" someone shouted.

Ezzy made a beeline for the beach. Luke went the other way, swimming toward the person who'd seen the shark. Once out of the water, Ezzy watched her little brother, thinking: *It's obvious who inherited the brains in the family.* She walked to her backpack and took out a towel to dry off. She decided it wasn't a bad start—at least she'd gotten in the water.

Luke and her father soon finished snorkeling. Luke removed his fins and ran toward his sister. "Ez, you should have seen the shark. It was this big." He spread his arms nearly as wide as they could go. "It was awesome!"

"Do you still have all your fingers and toes?" she asked.

He gave her a look like she'd just said puppies eat their owners.

"I think it was a white-tipped reef shark," their father noted. "It swam right under us."

"So cool!" Luke added.

"So sorry I missed it," Ezzy said sarcastically as her stomach growled loudly. "Is it lunchtime yet?"

"Yes, my always-starving-daughter, it's almost time for more food." Ezzy's father tousled Luke's hair. "This is just the beginning. We have a whole new excursion this afternoon. It's supposed to be one of the best hikes in the Galápagos. Tons of birds and other animals."

"Oh joy," Ezzy muttered. But then she saw the look on her father's face. "No, I mean, that'll be cool. Right, Luke?"

Luke pumped his head up and down so hard Ezzy thought he might snap a vertebra. Then he hugged her, saying, "We're going to have so much fun, Sis."

Ezzy smiled and hugged him back. She really did love the kid and knew how much the trip meant to him and her dad. For a week, she could stay calm and do the nature thing. She could be more like her mother and everyone else there—even if it killed her and, she swore, it just might.

Siesta Time

After a short zodiac ride back to the *Darwin Voyager*, the passengers showered and got ready for lunch. Ezzy, her brother and father made their way to the ship's dining room. Sunlight streamed in through a row of rectangular windows illuminating the large round tables lining the room. At the center was a buffet rich in food choices. A chef stood off to the side at a small counter making pasta to order.

Ezzy made her way around the buffet, filling her plate. She then sat at a table next to her brother. Staring at her food, she wondered where to begin. It was a smorgasbord of her favorites: a slice of pizza oozing cheese, a small juicy hamburger, and a helping of spaghetti and meatballs. In between her plate and Luke's was another dish piled high with French fries.

"Ezzy, I see you're going super healthy and really taking advantage of the theme of today's lunch," her father teased.

Having just taken a big bite of her burger, Ezzy chewed and smiled sheepishly. The lunch was designed to highlight the foods of Ecuador, the country that owned the Galápagos Islands. But Ezzy had avoided anything she didn't recognize and already like.

"How about trying some of this fish ceviche?" her dad suggested, pointing to his plate. "It's excellent and a local specialty."

Ezzy spied the pile of cut-up fish on his plate. It looked kinda slimy. "Is it raw?"

"It's soaked in lime juice. Almost as good as cooking it."

"Okay, so it *is* raw."

"C'mon, give it a try."

Luke stuck a French fry in his mouth and watched his sister closely, clearly waiting to see what she would do. Ezzy hesitated and then tentatively reached over with her fork and stabbed a small cubed piece of fish, thinking: *one bite—how bad can it be?* She closed her eyes and popped it into her mouth. Forget the taste, the texture was wet, cold, and just as she thought: *slimy.*

"Mmmm," Ezzy said to her father, trying not to make a this-is-the-most-disgusting-thing-I've-ever-eaten face. "Yummy." She turned to her brother. "You should try it."

Luke shook his head. "No thanks."

"I hope you'll both be a little more adventurous in your eating while you're here," her father added.

Luke nodded as he shoved another French fry into his mouth.

"You know your mother loved trying new things," he continued. "Remember all those new and sometimes odd recipes she used to try out on us?" He leaned closer, lowering his voice. "Some of them were pretty good, but other meals didn't quite make the mustard, if you know what I mean."

"Make the mustard?" Luke asked.

"Maybe it's pass the mustard."

"Pass the mustard?" Ezzy said. "What the heck does that mean?"

"Come to think of it," her father answered. "I'm not really sure." Changing the subject, he pulled out the daily program of activities they'd gotten in their cabins. As he ate, her father read about the afternoon's excursion, "Punta Suarez on Española Island is a true gem of the Galápagos, where wildlife viewing is at its very best. Large populations of Nazca and blue-footed *boobies* make their home here, as well as the majestic waved albatross."

Luke giggled when his dad said boobies, which made Ezzy laugh.

Their father smiled and continued reading, "The rocky trail is one and a half miles long and requires good balance. The hike will take us to the island's steep southern cliffs where a dramatic blowhole shoots water high into the sky. Española is the only island..."

Ezzy's attention drifted to the passengers sitting at the tables nearby. In addition to the crew, she thought there were about forty passengers aboard, including her family. At the table next to her were that guy Aiden, his twin sisters (who were currently taking selfies in front of the buffet), and his parents. Next to them were several elderly couples and one pair of preppy-looking slightly younger men. Ezzy couldn't see the rest of the people very well from where she sat. Mostly, they were all talking quietly and eating.

"So, what do you think?" her father asked. "This afternoon sounds amazing."

Luke bobbed his head in agreement and Ezzy faked a smile. "Sounds awesome."

Though they were both full to the brim, Luke and Ezzy couldn't help but check out the dessert table. As it turned out, Ecuador was famous for more than the Galápagos or ceviche. Its pastries and cakes were world renowned. Ezzy fell in love with a deliciously moist cream-laden cake called *tres leches*. She had two helpings and decided Ecuadorian food wasn't so bad after all.

Suffering from post-lunch food comas, her father and brother headed back to the cabin they shared. Ezzy was feeling very full too, but also buzzing from all the sugar she'd just consumed. She didn't feel like going to her cabin, so instead she decided to wander around the ship for a bit.

Ezzy took the stairs and strolled toward the back or stern of the ship. Going through the ship's lounge, she looked around. It was a popular place to hang out. The room was lined with tall windows through which you could see the dark blue ocean going by. Just below the windows were yellow couches fronted by small glass tables. In the center of the room stood a few more tables surrounded by matching, comfy, cushiony chairs. At the front of the lounge was a small dance floor and a big flat screen for presentations.

Staring at the room's decorations, Ezzy realized the theme—all things Darwin and Galápagos. A photo of a stuffy looking old white guy hung on one back wall. She was pretty sure it was Charles Darwin. On another wall was a giant map of the Galápagos. She counted about fifteen major islands. They straddled a line, which was labeled the equator. A small replica of a tall sailing ship sat in a corner of the lounge. A plaque nearby explained that it was Darwin's ship, *The Beagle*. Enlarged photographs of Galápagos wildlife also hung on the walls. One was of a giant tortoise. Ezzy figured it was one animal she'd have no problems with. After all, even she could outrun a giant tortoise.

A few other people were in the lounge. They were reading or looking at photos on their tablets, and one very unhappy looking man seemed to be trying to connect his computer to the Internet. The Wi-Fi onboard was pretty sketchy, and a cell phone signal was simply nonexistent.

Ezzy headed to the doorway leading to the open deck on the ship's stern. As she was passing through, the ship hit a wave and the deck tilted just enough to throw her off balance. She tripped over the lip at the base of the doorway, nearly running headfirst into someone coming the other way.

"Whoa! Watch your step, snorkel girl."

It was that boy, Aiden. *Oh great*, Ezzy thought. At least she hadn't fallen completely or landed on him. She steadied herself and pretended as if nothing had happened.

He turned quickly and followed her out. "Did you see the shark this morning?"

"Nope," she said, heading to the stern railing and trying to look like she was concentrating on the white bubbly wake streaming behind the ship. She didn't really want to talk to the guy. He was the one that made fun of her on the beach. Besides, what would she say?

"So, you here with your family?"

"Uh huh."

"I'm Aiden, by the way, from New York. I'm here with my parents and sisters. My folks are all over Darwin and the evolution thing. Dad gave me a book about the guy and his travels. I think it's called *Voyage of the Beagle*. Haven't read it yet."

He paused. Ezzy figured he was waiting for her to tell him something about herself. She continued to stare out at the ocean behind the ship. Not too far behind them was another ship. It was smaller than the *Darwin Voyager*. Ezzy figured it was probably another tourist boat. Who else would be out there? *Maybe they're pirates*, she thought jokingly.

"Hey, my parents gave me a GoPro to make a video of my Galápagos experience. I think they're hoping I'll get school credit. I can even take it underwater. You *are* afraid of the water, aren't you?"

"*No*," Ezzy said sharply, turning to him. She couldn't help but notice how his dark hair seemed perfectly messy and he had very deep blue eyes, almost the same color as the ocean.

"Just sayin' that's what it seemed like on the beach. And what's with the outfit, you wanna be a naturalist or something?"

He was referring to the clothes her father insisted they all wear—khaki shorts, a light-colored T-shirt, and hiking sandals. The outfit closely resembled the khaki shirts and shorts the naturalists all wore. Ezzy didn't even have on her matching floppy khaki hat.

"Geez," she said before turning and heading to the next deck up.

"What? Wait..."

Ezzy didn't stop to see how else the guy could insult her. Once on the next deck up, she headed to the bow. Thankfully, Aiden hadn't followed her. It's not like she needed him or anyone else to tell her that she was dorky as well as a wimp, given the whole wild animals thing.

At the railing, she stared ahead. Stored on the bow below, Ezzy could see a couple of the big zodiacs they used to get to and from shore. Ahead of the ship, the water was a bright royal blue. To the left was a small island blanketed by short green shrubs. Piles of black rock and narrow white sandy beaches lined the shore. Like the island they were on earlier, this one also appeared uninhabited. Ezzy couldn't remember the last time she'd been somewhere without paved roads, cars, and people on cell phones. It was very different from what she was used to where she lived, outside of Washington DC.

Then Ezzy noticed the noise—just the hum of the ship's engines and the wind rushing by. The air smelled salty and fresh. It seemed very peaceful. *Maybe too peaceful,* she thought. A weird feeling hit her and Ezzy shivered, looking around. Something didn't feel right. Ezzy shook her head; she was probably just nervous about the afternoon hike and all the wild, unpredictable animals they were sure to encounter. She took a deep breath, trying to relax and remember why she was there, for her family. She imagined her mother standing beside her, holding her hand. She could do this—hopefully.

After a while, Ezzy went back to her cabin. She had about an hour before the afternoon hike. She lay on the bed and looked at the book on the adjacent night table. Her dad had given both Luke and her a copy of Darwin's *Voyage of the Beagle.* Luke was thrilled. He'd done a book report on Charles Darwin in

school. Ezzy knew about Darwin of course, survival of
the fittest and everything. She had promised her dad
she'd read it but hadn't started yet.

Trailing Behind

While Ezzy lay on her bed, the nondescript sixteen-passenger boat continued to cruise slowly behind the *Darwin Voyager*. It was far enough away not to cause any concern by those on the larger ship. On the bridge two men spoke quietly.

"You're absolutely sure they won't take note of us following them?" asked the man, running his hand over his slicked-back hair.

"Leave it to me, Señor," answered the captain. "Our boat is like many others here in the islands. Even if they see us, they won't think twice about it."

"And there's a landing site on the island where we won't be seen?"

"Yes. I've lived and worked here for years. I know these islands extremely well. Haven't I proven that already?"

"I suppose so," the man replied. "But I'm paying you a lot for that, and your discretion of course."

"Yes, Señor, of course. Believe me, you'll get your money's worth."

The captain stayed on the boat's bridge, while the other man strode out a side door. He stared at the nearby island and glanced again at the larger ship ahead of them. He had invested a lot of money and time in his plan. It had taken him years to make all the right contacts, hire the right people, and to research what needed to be done. He had no doubt that this trip would be the start of a lucrative venture that would not only make him ultra-rich, but also gain him the respect of the scientific world.

Things had already gone so well, he needed another and bigger ship. The one ahead was perfect. It would play a key role in his plan, even though the passengers aboard didn't know it yet.

Española Spells Trouble

Later that afternoon, as their zodiac approached Española Island, Ezzy knew she was in trouble—big trouble. If the Galápagos was a week-long face-your-fears class about wild animals, this was going to be the all-too-soon final exam. Animals were everywhere—sea lions and marine iguanas were swimming in the shallow water near shore and resting on the sand, giant red crabs were crawling over the rocks, and squawking birds were flying all around overhead. While Ezzy tried not to hyperventilate or beg to be taken back to the ship, everyone else stared in wonder or whipped out their cameras.

Just landing on the island was going to be a challenge. A big sea lion lay snoozing on the small concrete pier they pulled up to. One after another, each person disembarked from the zodiac and crept calmly around it. Ezzy tried to do the same, cautiously approaching the sea lion. She heard a sound almost like a snore. She looked closer. It was a snore. The sea lion was sound asleep—and snoring. There was even sea lion drool dripping down its whiskered chin. That made her feel a little better, and she skirted carefully around the big furry fast-asleep fellow.

Their naturalist this time was Geovana, a thin, dark-haired woman with a pleasant smile and slight accent. "Head down the walkway to the beach," she told the group.

Walking down the concrete path, Ezzy almost stepped on a bright red crab the size of a cereal bowl. She leapt over the crab and nearly landed in a pile of marine iguanas. She ran down the path until she found an animal-free zone. Her heart was pounding and she was breathing hard. Luke walked happily down the trail, nearly skipping, and snickered at her.

"It's not funny."

Her father came over and tried to be comforting with a squeeze of Ezzy's shoulder. He then collected her life jacket to give to the zodiac driver. She couldn't believe her dad and Luke couldn't hear her heart, it was thumping so hard. Then again, they were too busy staring at the wildlife and taking photos—they were in animal heaven. Ezzy took a couple of deep breaths, willing herself to calm down. She could do this. She had to do it for her father and brother. She stepped closer to a pile of large iguanas nearby. They had surprising red and green splotches on their scaly skin and lay very still. Ezzy figured they were either seriously tired and just resting or deeply asleep. She couldn't tell which. Ezzy inched closer. Nothing happened. She looked around proudly, but no one seemed to notice her small act of bravery.

The group gathered around Geovana. Aiden and his family were there. His two sisters were dressed in white shorts and tight black halter-tops. Ezzy didn't think it looked very comfortable for hiking. She had on her family colors—khaki. She and Luke also carried small backpacks. Before they had left home, her father brought them to an adventure store to buy clothing and other stuff for the trip. He told the lady in the store they were going on a ship, so in addition to their hiking and snorkeling gear, she convinced him to buy all sorts of stuff related to boating. Ezzy didn't think they'd need half of it. Today, in his larger backpack, her father had packed a bottle of water along with insect repellent, a first-aid kit, his Swiss Army knife, their rain jackets, waterproof matches, and more.

Down the beach from where Ezzy stood, the selfie twins were trying to find the right angle so they both could be in a photo with a sea lion resting on the sand. Suddenly, one of the girls started screaming and hopping around. Ezzy looked to see what had happened and couldn't help but sympathize—the girl had stepped in some stinky sea lion surprise.

The other members of the hiking group included the two preppy guys Ezzy had seen at dinner. Both of them seemed dressed more appropriately for a round of golf rather than hiking through rough terrain. Ezzy hoped the men wouldn't slow them down. She wanted to get the hike over with as quickly as possible, as then there'd be less chance for any sort of wild animal incident—or freak-out. The other couple in the group didn't look like speedster hikers either. They made your stereotypical mid-western grandparents seem young and worldly. The elderly man and woman both had short spiky white hair and walked a bit hunched over. Ezzy thought their clothes looked very old-fashioned, noting in particular the high black socks the man wore with his sneakers. Though each did have a high-tech aluminum walking stick and a pretty snazzy lightweight backpack. When the older couple caught her staring at them, Grandma and Grandpa Jones (that's what Ezzy decided to call them) smiled sweetly and waved.

A small protected cove filled with clear turquoise water fronted the beach where the group gathered, and much of the island was blanketed by short green-leaved trees. On the airplane, Ezzy's father had told her that most of the islands in the Galápagos were actually volcanoes. But she didn't think the island they were on looked much like a volcano. It seemed relatively flat, with no sign of a cone-shaped mountain.

Ezzy heard giggling and turned to see Luke staring at three small furry brown heads that had popped up in a nearby rocky pool of water. Three sets of big round eyes stared curiously back at her brother. The sea lion pups soon began jumping playfully, somersaulting, and chasing one another. For stinky, potential biters, Ezzy had to admit they were pretty cute.

"Okay, everyone ready?" Geovana asked. "Española Island is one of the oldest islands in the Galápagos and packed with wonderful wildlife. Did you notice the unusual red and green color of the marine iguanas here? Not only are they the only marine iguanas in the world, this species is distinct to the island. The coloration gets brighter during breeding season."

"They remind me of Christmas," Grandma Jones noted.

"Oh, sweetie pie," Grandpa Jones added lovingly. "Everything reminds you of Christmas."

"Is that so bad, honey pie? It *is* the best time of the year."

Ezzy chuckled. If they weren't holding hands and staring adoringly at one another, she would have thought the couple were being sarcastic. But instead, it was sweet and a little comical.

Meanwhile, a bunch of plate-sized bright red crabs had crawled toward Luke and now he was surrounded by curious crustaceans.

Geovana noticed Luke's predicament. "Uh, just step over them and walk to me, young man. They're completely harmless."

Luke nodded and leapt calmly over the large crabs. Several marine iguanas nearby then sneezed in synchrony. Aiden aimed his GoPro at the iguanas as Geovana announced, "No worries, they're just sneezing out excess salt. As cold-blooded reptiles, they sit here during the day to warm up in the sun and periodically sneeze out salt."

"More iguana goobers," Ezzy muttered, trying to keep her Zen calmness and a fake smile going. *I can do this.*

"Okay, let's move on," Geovana announced. "Watch where you step and please stay on the trail."

Small black and white-painted sticks marked the rock-lined sandy trail. Luke wanted to hear everything Geovana said, so the Skylar family positioned themselves directly behind her. Aiden and his family followed, and the rest of the group trailed behind. Ezzy figured it would be a who-was-the-slowest contest between the sweet but elderly Joneses and the preppy golf guys.

At the top of a small hill, Geovana stopped. She pointed to a nearby pile of dark volcanic rocks. "Galápagos hawk!"

Ezzy turned. At eye-level and way too close for comfort was a large brown and yellow hawk—or as she thought of it, a large predatory bird with razor sharp talons and a beak for tearing flesh. It was so close she could see the hawk's feathers rustling in the breeze and its beady eyes staring at her. She stepped back and stayed as still as possible, all the while her brain was yelling *run... run away.* Ezzy took another deep breath. Her dad moved closer and put his arm around her shoulder, whispering, "You're doing great, Ez. Keep it up."

"The Galápagos Hawk is another endemic species, unique to the Galápagos, and the top predator on the island," Geovana said. "They like to find high places to perch on to look for prey."

Luke's eyes were as big as softballs, and he muttered, "It's so close."

Geovana must have heard him. "The animals here are used to us and know that we pose no threat, so they will get very close without being nervous or afraid."

"So cool," Luke said a little louder.

"Yeah, so cool," Ezzy groaned. Her dad gave her a squeeze.

"What do they eat?" Aiden asked, aiming his Go-Pro at Geovana. Ezzy ducked out of the way. She didn't like being on camera or in photographs. She'd always thought her face was overly round and her dark eyebrows were too bushy and close together. If they grew any more, she figured she was going to have one of those unibrows. At least the dorky hat she wore hid the frizzy brown hair now trying desperately to escape from her ponytail.

"The hawks will eat just about whatever they can catch, including chicks, baby iguanas, and lava lizards. They also like Galápagos snakes."

"Snakes?" Ezzy echoed.

"They're small, black snakes, non-venomous. We'll be lucky if we see one."

"Awesome," Luke said.

Geovana smiled at Luke and continued down the trail. Soon they came to another small beach. The naturalist stopped and waited for everyone to catch up and gather around. The two preppy guys were happily chatting and seemed to be having a good time. Behind them were the Joneses, slowly catching up.

"Everyone okay?" Geovana asked.

"Peachy pie," replied Grandma Jones as her husband wiped the sweat from his brow and gave a slow thumbs-up adding, "tip top."

"The small sea lions you see here resting on the beach are pups whose mothers are out fishing right now. They're still nursing, so they'll stay on the beach or play nearby in the water while she's out feeding."

One of the pups began making a noise somewhere between a puppy's bark and a goat's bleating.

Geovana continued, "That's one way the mothers identify the pups, through their bark. Also smell. It's one reason we don't touch the sea lions. We could change their scent and the mothers might not recognize them."

"How old are the pups?" someone asked.

"These are probably a couple of months old," Geovana answered. "They'll stay with their mothers for about a year and a half or so."

"What happens if the mother gets eaten by a *shark* or something?" Aiden questioned, filming again.

"Unfortunately," Geovana replied. "The pup will starve."

Luke's eyes grew wide. "Wouldn't the other sea lions help it?"

Ezzy was shocked: it wasn't like Luke to speak up in public. Especially since their mom had died.

"No," Geovana answered. "The other mothers won't adopt an abandoned pup. But that's nature. Along the trail you might see dead animals for one reason or another. Here we don't remove the dead animals..."

"Not like the road kill at home," Aiden added, interrupting.

"Exactly," Geovana said. "It's all part of the natural ecosystem. We can't interfere in the Galápagos, unless the problem is human-caused. Okay, the rest of the trail is quite rocky. Is everyone okay to continue on?"

Grandpa Jones gave an enthusiastic two thumbs up. "We're good to go."

"You know it, apple of my eye, filling of my tart," added his wife.

"We're game," said one of the golf buddies.

"If there are any birds or animals in the trail, please step quietly around them," Geovana added. "Those with walking sticks watch where you place them. And be sure to drink plenty of water. It's hot."

No need to tell Ezzy that. It was like a steam bath under her floppy hat as sweat trickled down her back. Sticky perspiration was another reason she thought observing wildlife virtually from the comfort of your own home was more appealing than this out-in-nature hiking thing.

As Luke twisted opened the top of his water bottle, a scruffy-looking bird swooped down and nearly took off his nose. It landed on his foot and he smiled. Ezzy stepped back, out of the peck and poop zone.

Geovana chuckled. "The mockingbirds here like to beg for water. Please don't give them any."

Luke wiggled his foot. The mockingbird took off and landed in the sand nearby. Luke reached down. Ezzy figured he was going to try to pet the feathered flying poop machine. Instead, he picked up a strange-looking short purple stick and showed it to Geovana. "What's this?"

Geovana took the inch-and-a-half long cylindrical purple stick from Luke. "Good eyes. Anyone know what it is?"

The only replies were looks of bewilderment.

"This is the spine of a pencil urchin. When the pencil urchin dies, the spines fall off and wash up on the beach. Here in the Galápagos, the spines help create sand on some of the islands."

Examining the beach more closely, Ezzy realized that hundreds, maybe thousands of the purple spines littered the beach. Another dangerous sea creature she hadn't even thought of—sea urchins. Those spines could poke your eye out. And with so many on the beach, she figured there must be a ton of them in the ocean.

Geovana then stuck the dull end of the spine against her skin. "No worries about these. As kids, here in the Galápagos, we used to use them to draw. The spines are made of calcium carbonate, which is similar to chalk."

There's at least one less thing to worry about, Ezzy thought with relief, *being stuck by a pencil urchin spine.* She put her water bottle in her backpack, preparing to go. Suddenly, Luke grabbed her arm. He had on odd expression on his face. "Did you feel that?"

"Feel what?"

Luke pointed to the sea lions and iguanas. "Look." The sea lions on the beach were all awake and glancing around nervously. Pups called for their mothers, and the iguanas appeared restless, sneezing one after another. And down by the water, a herd of crabs scuttled over the black rocks.

"They must have felt it too," Luke said.

"Felt what?" Ezzy asked again.

"The shaking."

"What shaking?"

"The ground," Luke responded.

"I didn't feel anything."

Luke shrugged. Ezzy glanced about. The sea lions were already back to snoozing and no one else seemed to have noticed anything. And her father said she was the one with the vivid imagination. Ezzy looked around again. One of the zodiac drivers was revving his boat's outboard engine. It looked like he was fixing something. Maybe that had caused some weird vibration that had scared the animals and Luke felt it; he'd always been a sensitive kid.

"Let's keep going," Geovana said as she turned to continue down the trail. "Keep your eyes out for small birds. Those are Darwin's finches."

Luke ran happily after the naturalist. His father scurried after him and Ezzy followed more slowly. The path was now filled with large gray rocks.

"Take your time," Geovana instructed. "Watch your step and be careful. The paperwork on injuries and falls is murder." She winked at Luke.

Ezzy knew one footfall out of place now and she'd do an embarrassing face-plant. She tried to focus and not think about anything except navigating the rocky path and staying upright.

Geovana stopped to show Luke a small, striped male lava lizard moving its head and body up and down. "It's doing push-ups to attract a female."

Ezzy spied a wide flat rock. She stepped on it to watch the romantic calisthenics of the lizard. But the rock wasn't as stable as it looked. It teetered and seesawed precariously. As she started to fall, someone from behind reached a hand out to help. Ezzy instinctively grabbed it and steadied herself. She then looked back at the person, muttering an embarrassed, "Thanks."

Aiden grinned at her. "No problem. What's your name anyway? Since I did just save you."

"Hardly," she replied. After a pause, she added, "Ezzy. My name is Ezzy."

"Nice to officially meet you, Ezzy."

Behind him, his sisters giggled.

With her heart once again racing, Ezzy focused her attention back on the trail. She snuck a quick peek back at Aiden. Unlike her, he maneuvered easily across the rocks. It made her feel all the more awkward. She thought of her mother who used to tell her all the time that she just needed more self-confidence. Ezzy thought she needed some basic coordination skills.

After about ten minutes or so, they came to an opening in the bushes lining the trail. Geovana stopped and Ezzy discovered they were about twenty feet from the edge of a steep cliff. She hadn't even realized they'd been going up. Overhead, several fast, noisy white birds with long tail feathers flew by. Naturally she ducked. To Ezzy's surprise, no one else seemed to even notice the birds or the obvious potential for poop bombs. It was probably because their attention was focused on what was on the ground beside the trail.

A two-foot tall bird stood on the packed reddish dirt. It had bright, extraordinarily blue feet. They were the brightest, bluest feet Ezzy had ever seen. Then again, she'd never seen anything with big blue webbed feet. The bird's feet were so blue they looked fake— as if someone had dumped brilliant sky-blue paint all over them. Even she knew what kind of bird it was.

The blue-footed booby stood very still, staring at the group. It had a white chest, brown wings and bill, and a mottled head with big light-colored eyes. Suddenly, the bird tilted its head back, lifted its wings and tail, and whistled—a sharp, distinct whistle.

"That's the male," Geovana told the group. "It's skypointing to attract females flying overhead. The females are a bit bigger and they honk instead of whistle. That's one way you can tell them apart." She made a funny honking sound and the blue-footed booby stared curiously at her. Ezzy figured it must have been a pretty good imitation.

Just then a blue-footed booby flew by and the male skypointed and whistled again. Ezzy's father was in photo bliss and Luke was again mesmerized. Another blue-footed booby landed on a rock nearby. Its feet were almost purplish blue.

Geovana whispered, "That's a female."

The male blue-footed booby turned to the female and slowly raised one big blue foot. Then it put the foot down, swayed to the side, and picked up the other, and then did it again. The female joined in. They were... dancing.

Ezzy thought the birds looked goofy raising and lowering their big blue feet and waddling around. It made her think again of her mother. She would have loved the booby dance! Her mom used to dance in the living room to old songs with Ezzy's dad. She was always trying to get Ezzy to join in. At that moment, Ezzy really wished her mother was there with them. Her throat tightened, and tears threatened to well up.

Ezzy then noticed Luke. He was grinning so widely, his cheeks looked even pudgier and cuter than usual. He started to giggle. It was such a joyful sound that everyone turned to watch, and smiles broke out all around. Her father began to laugh, and instead of crying, Ezzy broke out in a real, honest-to-goodness grin. This trip was going to be really good for Luke and her dad—as long as she didn't ruin it. She moved a little closer to the birds.

"They're courting," Geovana told the group quietly.

"It's better than the Macarena," her father said, still chuckling.

Luke and Ezzy rolled their eyes. The male booby bent down and picked up a small twig. It presented it to the other bird and placed it on the ground nearby.

"He's saying I can make a fantastic nest for you," Geovana added softly. "They don't create a nest with sticks or anything; it's just part of a ritual. The nest will be a packed circular section on the ground surrounded by guano—also known as bird poop. The female will lay one or two eggs right on the dirt."

A few minutes later, Geovana told the group to move on. But Luke was so taken with the blue-footed boobies, the Skylars let the others go ahead so they could watch a little longer. Before he left, Aiden stood in front of the birds filming. "Here's the blue-footed booby doing its mating dance. Gotta love *boobies!*"

"Aiden!" his mother said. "This is supposed to be an educational video for school."

"What?" he asked innocently.

He turned to Ezzy and winked.

"Lame," she whispered as he passed by.

Soon the trail opened up onto a wide flat area of packed dirt surrounded by gray rocky cliffs. Geovana halted and gathered the group together. She was about to start talking, but stopped abruptly and looked around, appearing puzzled.

"Honey, is something wrong?" asked Grandma Jones.

Geovana scratched her head. "See those white and black birds over there?" She pointed to several big white birds with black wings sitting atop the rocks by a cliff. They had yellowish beaks and a mask of black around their faces. "Those are Nazca boobies, and this place should be teeming with them. I've never seen so few here."

Luke must have been feeling shy again because he tugged on his father's shorts and whispered to him.

"Where'd they go?" his father asked.

"That's an excellent question," Geovana answered.

Before she could say anything else, a head popped up from below the cliff ahead of the group—a human head that is. It was another naturalist leading a small group in the opposite direction. "¡Hola!"

Ezzy figured maybe they were from the other boat she'd seen.

Geovana waved. "Hola, Manuel."

The other naturalist was a tall wiry guy who looked like he could run a marathon without breaking a sweat. He stopped to help his group up the cliff trail. And they clearly needed help. Three sweaty red-faced men climbed up and over the cliff edge. They wore sweat-stained polo shirts, well-worn shorts, and baseball hats pulled down low over their faces. One of the men, a rather ordinary looking, slightly overweight middle-aged fellow, had fallen. Blood ran down one leg, and he had a bandage wrapped around his knee. Helping him along was a tall, skinny man with stringy black hair and a droopy mustache. The third guy followed. He was a burly dude with a goatee and sour expression. Ezzy didn't think the men looked much like the wildlife enthusiasts one might expect in the Galápagos Islands. Then again, she was there. Besides, her mother always said looks can be deceiving and that she shouldn't be too quick to judge people. Still, they didn't look like your average I-can't-wait-to-hike-through-the-wilderness kind of guys.

"Everything okay?" Geovana asked.

"We'll make it back," the naturalist answered. "You guys have a doctor onboard, right?"

Geovana nodded and pulled a small radio from her pocket. "You want me to tell them you'll be stopping by?"

The man with the injured leg stood up straighter. "No need for that. Just a little fall is all. I'm fine."

The other naturalist shrugged.

"Okay," Geovana said. "But call if you need help."

After the other group left, they drank some water and continued on. The trail snaked down the cliff ahead, crossed a rocky cove, and then climbed another small cliff. A few sea lions lay on the rocks and further along the trail were more blue-footed boobies. A couple of hawks circled overhead.

So far, Ezzy thought things were going well. She hadn't been attacked and hadn't freaked out. She'd bravely approached the iguanas and gotten a little closer to the blue-footed boobies. Maybe she could actually do this nature hiking thing, even without her mother.

Reptiles Fly

The hiking trail on Española had flattened out and become less rocky. A low growing plant resembling a shaggy red carpet blanketed the area. Soon the group arrived at the edge of a high rocky cliff overlooking the ocean. A vast expanse of deep blue water lay offshore, with long swells rolling toward the island. No other land was in sight. As Ezzy leaned over the cliff to see what lay below, her father grabbed onto the back of her shorts.

"I'm fine, *Dad*."

Her father pulled her back from the edge. "Yeah, but let's not give your old dad here a heart attack, please."

Ezzy peeked over the cliff edge, from a little farther back this time. Below was a wide shelf of black rock.

An incoming wave struck the rock and a deep thump rang out. A towering plume of seawater shot skyward like a giant geyser creating a spray of seawater that doused the group. Ezzy wiped her face, enjoying the refreshing coolness of the mist.

"Voila!" announced Geovana. "Enjoy your Galápagos shower. This is the famous blowhole. Incoming waves force water into a fracture in the rocks below and it shoots up."

"How's my hair, sweetie?" Grandma Jones asked her husband, patting it with exaggeration.

"As lovely as ever, honey," he laughed.

Luke's eyes got big as he pointed to the rocky shelf below the cliff. "Look, dad. There's an iguana down there."

"Uh oh," Geovana said.

"Uh oh, what?" Ezzy asked.

Before the naturalist could answer, another big wave hit. A giant plume of seawater shot up, and with it went a very surprised marine iguana. As if blasted from a cannon, the black creature flew through the air, wriggling its legs. An instant later it plummeted to the ground, landing with a thud on the rocks nearby. The iguana righted itself and sat still as if in a daze. Seconds later, the creature scurried away.

It had happened so fast, Ezzy hadn't had time to scream, run, or even duck. She was immediately grateful that she hadn't been in the landing zone or it would have definitely been humiliation freak-out time.

Geovana laughed. "This is the only place we've ever seen iguanas fly. But don't worry, folks, they're very hardy creatures. They don't get hurt."

"I think I got it on camera," Aiden told the group.

They sat on the rocks above the blowhole for a while, resting and enjoying the cool spray. Ezzy stayed wary, on the lookout for flying iguanas. The selfie twins were trying to get a shot with the water gushing up behind them, but the timing was hard to predict, and every time they got wet the two girls screeched and jumped out of the shower zone.

"Hey, Ezzy," Aiden shouted. "Wanna shoot me with the blowhole in the background for my film?"

"No, thanks. Get your sisters to do it. They seem pretty good with a camera."

"Oh, c'mon. It'll just take a minute, and this way I can explain how it works while you film."

Ezzy's dad gave her a gentle shove from behind. "Go ahead, Ez."

She rose reluctantly and climbed over the rocks to Aiden.

"Okay, just press this button and aim it toward me, like this."

"Got it."

"Make sure you've got me and the blowhole in the frame."

"I got it."

"And don't cut off my head."

"Do you want my help or not?"

"Yeah, yeah. Okay, get ready."

Ezzy held the camera up and pushed the start button. "Uh... action." Aiden started describing where they were and the blowhole. It was kinda boring. "Tell the flying iguana story," she whispered.

He nodded and explained how a marine iguana had just flown through the air. Then he said to pan the camera around to see the group and the rest of the island. Ezzy moved the camera around. Aiden grabbed her hand. "Not so fast, you'll make the audience motion sick."

His fingers were hot and sweaty. Her stomach lurched. "Here, you do it," she said, backing away.

"Sure, okay, if you don't want to."

"Yeah, no big deal." Ezzy headed back to her family. Her father was grinning at her.

"What?"

"I'm glad you're making friends."

Luke nodded and raised his eyebrows. She smacked him lightly on the head. "C'mon, looks like we're heading out."

The next section of the path was treacherous. Big, dark, irregularly-shaped rocks filled the trail. The only way ahead was to step from one rock to the next.

"Please be very careful here," Geovana told the group. "This is the most common place for falls, and it's a long way back to carry someone. Take your time."

When it was Ezzy's turn to enter the big rock danger zone, she stepped up onto the first rock in the trail. Her legs felt a little noodle-like and shaky. She took a deep breath and peered ahead. Luke was already scrambling across the rocks, followed by Aiden. Her father noticed her hesitation and stopped to help. She was about to take his hand when she noticed Aiden watching. "Thanks, Dad, but I can do this."

Ezzy wiped the sweat from her eyes and carefully stepped onto the next rock. Its surface was angled, but the thick-soled sandals she wore gripped the rock tightly. She moved ahead slowly, looking for the flattest surfaces possible and using her arms for balance. On one pointy rock, Ezzy teetered dangerously. To avoid falling, she leapt onto a big, square rock nearby. Soon she was through the worst of it and the trail turned back to packed sand. Ezzy breathed a sigh of relief. She hadn't fallen and was proud that she'd made it through without help. Her father smiled and gave her a thumbs up.

Looking back down the trail, Ezzy saw the elderly Joneses going slowly, but surprisingly steadily, over the rocks. She hoped they wouldn't fall.

A few minutes later, Geovana stopped at another opening in the short bushy trees lining the path. She pointed to a large, open and flat grassy area. It ran all the way back to the cliffs. "This is the albatross airport. Where the albatross come in to land and then go to the cliff to take off."

Two birds emerged from behind some bushes.

They were large, nearly three feet tall. Each had a long skinny white neck, a big triangular head, lengthy yellow bill, and a thick brown body. As they walked across the grass, the birds' heads rocked weirdly from side to side, almost like they were too heavy for their necks.

"The waved albatross are very large birds," Geovana noted.

No joke, Ezzy thought.

"They spend years out at sea and then fly in to mate and lay their eggs."

"How come there are only two?" Aiden asked.

Geovana looked around as if deciding what to say. "Last week there were more. They might be off fishing right now, I guess."

Aiden aimed his GoPro at the albatross. "Folks, we have another bird mystery on our hands. Where are all the albatross?"

The two large birds waddled toward one another. When they were about two feet apart, they lowered their heads and bowed. It was like a bird how-do-you-do. Next, they rose up to their full height and snapped their bills wide open, facing each other. The albatross then whacked their long bills together, like in a sword fight. A clacking sound rang out.

"Are they fighting?" Aiden asked.

"No, that's their courtship display," Geovana announced. "The waved albatross has one of the most astonishing courtship rituals in the world. Scientists think they mate for life. However, through studying the genetics of the chicks, we've discovered that they also have little romances on the side. We think sneaky males jump in for a little action before the true mates land."

Ezzy turned to Luke. He was wide-eyed and staring at the birds with a look of amazement and simple pure joy. Smiling, he waddled around and bowed to her as if he was an albatross. Ezzy grinned and bowed back as her father and the rest of the group laughed.

Ezzy turned back to watch the giant birds. Seeing the albatross waddle, bow, and whack their bills together was unexpected, but not in a scary or creepy way. She glanced over to her father and Luke. They were having a great time.

At the side of the trail, Grandma Jones was talking quietly with Geovana. Ezzy wondered if the elderly couple would need help getting back to the ship. If she was sweating and tired, they must have been exhausted. Geovana pointed to a cluster of small trees and the Joneses headed that way.

Ezzy stared, wondering where they were going until her father pulled her aside. "It's not polite to stare. I think they're going on a bathroom break."

"Oh."

Once the couple returned, the group continued on. Only a few rocks now littered the trail. But it was still hot, and soon there were bugs, lots of bugs. A cloud of gnats buzzed around Ezzy's head. She swatted at them and clamped her mouth shut. No bug snacks for her. Ahead, something bigger flitted across the trail. Luke ran over to see what it was. Ezzy didn't want to see or know what was there. As she maneuvered around her brother, an enormous insect leapt from the ground, nearly landing on her. She flinched and ran ahead. "Ick!"

"It's just a grasshopper, Sis," Luke said, looking at one of the biggest bugs Ezzy had ever seen, now perched on his arm. The thing was almost the length of her hand and so large she could see its round black bug-eyes, multicolored beetle-hard body, icky waving antennas, and bent-up lengthy legs. Ezzy didn't need to see anymore. She hurried down the trail. But soon there were grasshoppers jumping all around her. She let out a yelp, sprinted ahead, and nearly tripped.

Ezzy stopped and tried to collect herself. *They're just bugs, just bugs.* Her pulse was racing. She took a deep breath and looked back. The bug had jumped off Luke's arm and everyone else walked along seemingly unperturbed by the leaping, disturbingly large insects. She started down the trail trying to pretend that everything was fine, and she hadn't just had a minor freak-out.

As they came out of the trees at the coast, two things lifted Ezzy's spirits: A cool breeze that blew away the bugs and seeing the ship anchored in the distance. They were close to the landing site. The hike was almost over and with the exception of the recent small, big-bug incident, she'd done well, better than she'd expected.

Luke yanked on her arm and pointed overhead. "Look, another hawk and it's got something!"

Ignoring him and the hawk, Ezzy stared at the ground and kept walking. However, something must have startled the hawk overhead and it released its catch, or perhaps the thing squirmed free. Either way, it fell like a living, wriggling bomb from the sky, hurtling downward. And when the writhing black snake landed, it landed... right on Ezzy's head. The snake slid, still squirming, off her hat and onto her shoulder before bouncing to the ground.

"Aargh!" Ezzy sprinted down the trail, feeling like the long scaly creature was still on her. She shivered in disgust. Once she was far away from the drop zone, Ezzy stopped, shaking and gasping for air.

When her father, Luke, and Geovana caught up to her, between gasps, Ezzy announced, "No more birds, iguanas, bugs or snakes... I'm done. No more nature. That's it. I'm staying on the ship from now on."

"Calm down, Ez," her father said. "You're fine."

"It was just a little snake," Luke added.

She sneered at her brother. "Nope, that's it. I'm done."

"Let's get you back to the ship," Geovana suggested. Ezzy swore the naturalist was trying not to laugh. That didn't make her feel any better. She didn't think if a snake had landed on Geovana's head, she'd be laughing. It could have bitten her, or she could have had a heart attack. Enough. For the rest of the trip, she'd be sticking to the ship. No more creepy, potentially deadly wild animals, giant flying grasshoppers or hikes over seesawing rocks. She would be just fine with seeing the rest of the Galápagos from the comfort and safety of the *Darwin Voyager*.

Island Recon

Most of the men had avoided being seen. Few boats had been around and not too many people were on the island. They had landed on some rocks hidden by an overgrowth of mangroves. It was not an official visitor site. After a reconnaissance hike around the island, the operation had begun. The men now had some work to do offshore, but planned to return for a few more hours later, after dark.

The man in charge was pleased. His plan was working even better than he'd imagined. A few more days and he'd not only be on the road to riches, but also fame and admiration. He envisioned what his life of wealth would be like and how he would accept the prestigious awards he was sure to win.

Nighttime in the Galápagos

That evening, Ezzy caught several people glancing her way and snickering. No one had mentioned the snake incident, but word must have spread around the ship about her unfortunate reptile-from-the-sky encounter. Ezzy didn't think the other passengers would think it was funny if it had happened to them. She was still set on her plans—not to go anywhere near anything slithering, with wings, claws, or fins any time soon. She'd just have to accept her issue with wild animals and that she wasn't as much like her mother as she (and her father) had hoped.

After the briefing for the next day's excursions, they went to dinner. Ezzy sat quietly, while her father and Luke did all the talking. They recounted the hike and described all the animals they'd seen. Luke repeatedly peeked over at his sister, looking about ready to burst. Finally, when he clearly couldn't hold it in any longer, he blurted out, "And you should have seen your face, Ez, when that snake fell on you." Luke nearly doubled over laughing. Others in the room turned to see what was so hilarious.

Ezzy felt her face get hot. She glared at her brother. "It's not funny."

"No harm done, Ez," her father said. "Besides, you did great. When the going gets tough, the tough run up the trail."

She gave them a disgusted grunt, got up, and stomped away from the table.

"We're just kidding, Ez," her father called out. "Come back."

Ezzy didn't even turn around. She headed up the stairs and outside to the open deck at the ship's stern. If she weren't so angry, she might have cried. Then she looked up. "Whoa!"

The sky was bursting with stars. Back home, Ezzy had seen stars, but nothing like this. It was the twinkling night sky at home on steroids.

Next thing she knew, Luke and her father were at her side.

"We were just kidding, Sis," Luke said sweetly.

Her father put his arm around her, gave Ezzy a comforting squeeze, and looked upward, following her gaze. "Quite the show tonight."

Luke also turned skyward. "Awesome!" He pointed to an especially dense band of stars. "Is that the Milky Way?"

"I believe it is," his father answered. "Without the lights of civilization, here you can see what the night sky really looks like."

Ezzy hadn't really thought about how much difference all the lights of cities and towns make. Soon, a bright speck of light shot across the backdrop of shimmering stars. "I think I just saw a shooting star."

As she stood watching the stars with her father and brother, Ezzy's anger subsided. In her heart, she knew her family didn't mean to hurt her feelings. Ezzy thought about how sometimes when people think they're just joking, it can be hurtful. She made a mental note to herself to remember that for the future.

When her neck got sore from staring upward, Ezzy glanced over the side of the ship toward the bow. At first, she thought she was seeing things—too many stars on the brain. But then she looked again and pointed. "Dad, there's some kind of light out there in the ocean. See, it's red and I think it's flashing."

"Where?"

"Right there," she said pointing again. "There are a couple of red lights. And I swear, I'm not imagining it."

Her father squinted, staring out into the dark. "Ez, I think you're right."

Just then Geovana happened by. "It's a perfect night for stargazing!"

Ezzy pointed at the ocean. "Geovana, what are those red lights out there?"

The naturalist cupped her hands around her eyes and stared in the direction Ezzy was pointing. "¡Oh, *mierda*¡"

She didn't speak Spanish, but Ezzy didn't think the naturalist was saying oh happy day.

Geovana ran to a phone on a wall nearby. She grabbed it and spoke rapidly in Spanish. After hanging up, she came running back. "Do you still see the lights?"

They peered out into the night's darkness. The ship began to slow. It then started turning. In the distance, Ezzy could still see a glimpse of red underwater.

"What is it?" her father asked.

"An illegal fishing net," Geovana groaned. "Fishermen sink the net and use the red lights so they can relocate it at night and haul in their catch. It's a terrible way to fish. The net catches everything that swims into it, including sea turtles, sharks, and even dolphins. Sometimes they run the catch offshore to a ship waiting outside the marine reserve or they'll try to sell it as legally caught in the markets.

"But thanks to you," she continued. "I just reported it to the captain. He's going to come around to get a better fix on the location and then he'll call the park authorities."

"What'll they do?" Ezzy asked.

Geovana shrugged. "We're a long way out and they don't have a lot of boats, but if possible, they'll come and pull out the net."

As the ship turned around, Luke tugged on his father's pant leg and pointed to another light in the distance. It was yellow and seemed to be floating above the sea.

Geovana noticed where the boy was pointing. "Looks like another ship, probably at anchor for the night."

They watched as the *Darwin Voyager* made a slow circle around the submerged lights marking the illegal fishing net. The other ship remained stationary. Ezzy figured it was probably another tourist boat, but then another possibility came to mind—the fishermen who'd set the illegal net.

Quiet Time Goes Bad

The ship cruised through the night. Ezzy knew because a nightmare woke her up. It was about snakes falling from the sky. When she realized this time it was only a dream, Ezzy relaxed, but still it took a while for her to fall back asleep.

At breakfast the next morning, Ezzy informed her father that she still had no intention of going on a hike, snorkel excursion, or whatever creepy creature escapade was planned for that day. He and Luke tried their best to change her mind. Her dad pulled out all the stops with the faulty sayings; suggesting she was stubborn as a cat, making a mountain out of a mice hole, and that she needed to get back on the donkey.

"Donkey? What does that have to do with it?" Ezzy asked.

"I think he means horse," Luke corrected, smiling.

"Exactly," her father added. "You know when you fall off something, you need to get back on to get over it."

"Not going to happen," she said.

Luke and her father continued trying to convince her.

Finally, when she'd had enough, Ezzy relented. "Okay, okay. How about if I stay onboard this morning and go out in the afternoon?" Though she seriously doubted that would happen.

"I don't know," her father replied. "I'm not crazy about leaving you onboard by yourself."

"C'mon, dad," Ezzy said. "I'm not a little kid anymore. Besides, what could happen? It's not like I can go anywhere, and there's plenty of crew people around."

Her father pursed his lips, looking skeptical.

Ezzy yawned and stretched her arms wide. "Besides, I didn't sleep well, and this will give me a chance to rest and I can even read that book about Darwin you gave me."

Her father hesitated. "Okay. I guess you can stay aboard this morning. Besides, as you said, what could happen?"

A little later, as the rest of the passengers loaded into the zodiacs with the naturalists, Ezzy stood on the stern watching, one deck up. Luke waved as they headed to shore with Jorge in one of the boats. Aiden and his family were there too. He looked up at Ezzy questioningly and then turned to her father.

As the zodiacs headed for the island, Ezzy glanced around. It was empty and quiet on the back deck. It felt like she had the whole ship to herself. Ezzy let out a long sigh of relief. She could finally relax and not worry about doing anything stupid, embarrassing or uncoordinated.

She headed into the lounge. One of the crew members noticed her and came over. "Miss, how come you're not out on the excursion? Did you miss the boat? Would you like me to see if we can call them back?"

"No, I'm fine."

"Are you sure? I bet I could arrange for you to still go."

"No thanks. I'm okay."

"My name's Carlos. If you change your mind just let me know. I'd be happy to help you get off the ship. Are you sure you don't want to go?"

Ezzy shook her head and walked away, thinking the guy was being kinda pushy. She stopped to look at the big map of the Galápagos on the wall. From behind her came a deep, gravelly, and distinctive voice, "Staying onboard, Señorita?"

Not this again, she thought. When Ezzy turned to assure whoever it was that she was truly fine with staying onboard, she was surprised to see the captain. She recognized him from the first evening on the ship when he had welcomed all the guests. He looked exactly like she expected a captain should look: older, stocky, with short gray-streaked hair and a matching beard.

"Uh huh," Ezzy kind of squeaked out.

"We keep you busy here in the Galápagos," he said. "But Señorita, are you sure you want to miss out on the trip this morning? I have connections." He winked. "You can still go."

What's with these people, Ezzy thought. Seemed like everyone wanted her to get off the ship or something. "No, thanks, I'm fine. Just taking a break."

"*Sí*, if you're sure."

"I am."

He turned to the map. "You know where we are on it?"

She shook her head. "Not really."

Now beside her, the captain pointed to the largest island on the map. "This is Isabela. Some say it looks like seahorse." He chuckled gruffly. "*Sí*, maybe a seahorse carrying a *grande* load."

Ezzy laughed. He was exactly right. The top half of the island looked like a skinny seahorse, but below that was a big round section of land as if it was hanging from the seahorse's butt.

The captain then pointed to a spot on the lower left side of the island. "We're *aquí*, here on the southwest side of Isabela. It is very remote, not many boats come this way and few people live on Isabela. There is one village, Puerto Villamil, *aquí.*" He pointed to the southeastern tip of the island. "Isabela, she is also one of the most active islands."

"Active? You mean like in volcanoes and erupting?"

"*Sí.* Last year, Wolf Volcano, *aquí* on Isabela, erupted." He pointed to the northern tip of the island, essentially in the middle of the seahorse's head. "*Más grande* surprise because we expected the next eruption to be *aquí,* here, on Fernandina."

He pointed to a smaller round island. It was the only island to the west of Isabela.

The captain continued, "We were *muy* lucky to see the eruption and make detour. It was *espectacular!* People on the ship got an *excelente* treat. Eruptions here draw lots of attention. Ships, they cruise by to watch and the Park sends rangers to the site."

"Uh... how often do the volcanoes here erupt?" Ezzy asked, thinking of Luke and her dad out hiking. "I mean, what about the people on the islands?"

"No worry. Volcanoes they erupt not so often. *Sí,* some lava, but nothing too *peligroso*—dangerous. And no one lives where the eruptions happen."

"But if that last eruption happened someplace unexpected, how do you know one won't happen where someone is? Like my mom used to say, it could be a science surprise."

The captain stroked his beard. "*Sí*. But honestly Señorita, no worry about our volcanoes. We'll be lucky if one erupts. Besides, we get alerts about any activity... and earthquakes."

"Earthquakes?" Ezzy repeated. She remembered that on their hike yesterday, Luke thought he felt the ground shake.

The captain nodded. "*Sí*, more earthquakes here than volcanoes erupting. Sometimes the earthquakes are related to eruptions."

"You mean if there's an earthquake, it could mean a volcano is about to erupt?"

The captain shook his head. "Mmmm maybe, but maybe no."

Ezzy stared at the man, not sure what to think.

"Now I must go see my engineer about a ship." He winked again and walked toward the stern.

Thinking about earthquakes and volcanoes, Ezzy headed to her cabin. Maybe Luke really did feel the ground shake yesterday. Did that mean a volcano was about to erupt? As if flying snakes and other dangerous wild creatures weren't enough, now she also had to worry about earthquakes and lava-spewing volcanoes. *Geez.*

Ezzy arrived at her cabin and was about to go in when she heard a commotion down the passageway. She turned to see two of the ship's officers running toward the stern. Ezzy wondered what was going on. With her curiosity aroused and little else to do, she followed. They went through a door marked "crew only".

Ezzy went up the stairs and through the lounge, reaching the railing on the stern deck just in time to see a zodiac approaching the platform below. At first, she thought something must have happened on the island and it was one of their boats returning. But then she realized it wasn't one of the *Darwin Voyager's* boats, which were black. This zodiac was gray. She turned to the nearby island. It stretched for miles and in the distance, she could see a towering cloud-covered peak. They were anchored too far away to see where the hikers or the ship's zodiacs were. But to her left lay another ship, smaller than the *Darwin Voyager*. The zodiac had to be from there.

Voices drifted up from below and Ezzy leaned over to see what was going on. The officers she'd seen moments ago were on the stern platform watching the approaching zodiac. One was a woman carrying a first-aid kit. Ezzy figured she was the ship's doctor.

The approaching zodiac carried four men. As soon as the boat's bow nudged the back platform, two of the men helped another man, who appeared injured, out of the zodiac. At first, Ezzy didn't recognize any of them, but then she realized one of the men assisting the injured guy was Manuel, the naturalist they'd seen on the hike yesterday. Ezzy looked closer. The injured guy was the middle-aged man who'd fallen. Maybe he was hurt worse than they'd thought. A wide bandage wrapped around his knee, and it looked like he couldn't put any weight on his leg. Ezzy listened as the ship's doctor addressed the injured man in Spanish. He quickly interrupted her, saying, "Sorry, no habla español."

"Señor, when did you injure your leg? Can you walk on it?"

"I..."

Then Ezzy heard a sharp gasp. "What in the...?"

"Quiet," ordered one of the men below. Ezzy couldn't see who it was. "Don't move or say another word. Give me your radios."

That doesn't sound good, thought Ezzy. There was a long pause in the conversation. She cautiously leaned further over to get a better look at what was going on, but they'd stepped back and out of view.

"Now, let's go see the captain. And no funny business, or you and this gentleman here will be taking a little swim with the sharks."

That definitely doesn't sound good. Ezzy heard them moving on the platform below toward the stairs. They were headed up to where she was standing. Searching for a place to hide, she spotted another door labeled "crew only." With no other obvious choice, she ran for it and slipped through. It led to a short narrow empty corridor lined with storage cabinets and what looked like refrigerators. She stood silently for a few moments trying to decide what to do next. No one had followed her or come into the corridor, so a few minutes later, driven by curiosity, Ezzy crept back to the door and cracked it open just enough to see through.

The first person up the stairs was one of the men from the other ship's zodiac. It was the burly goatee dude from the hike. He wore dark shorts and a khaki shirt like the naturalists, and had a towel draped over his bulging forearm. The sun glinted off something just poking out from under the towel. Ezzy caught a glimpse of what appeared to be dark metal. It looked like the tip of something, maybe a... a gun. She gasped and then slapped her hand over her mouth, afraid they might hear her. Ezzy's heart thumped like thunder in her ears.

The big goatee guy glanced around and then turned to watch as the others came up the stairs. The doctor was next, helping the injured man. Both appeared scared and confused. Behind them came the naturalist Manuel and then the other officer from the *Darwin Voyager*. At their heels was the other man from the zodiac. He was the other guy Ezzy had seen on the hike—the skinny man with the droopy mustache. He wore clothes similar to the big guy and also had a towel draped over one arm, which he pointed at the group.

The last man stared at the others, stroked his mustache lovingly and, in a slow drawl, said, "Okay, nice and easy. No mistakes and no one will get hurt. Are all the passengers off the ship?"

The *Darwin Voyager's* officer turned to the man hesitantly. "I believe so."

"Okay then, keep going."

They headed into the lounge, and Ezzy slumped to the floor. Her mind was racing a million miles a minute. *What's going on? What do they want?* Her heart hammered in her chest and sweat trickled down her forehead. She took a couple of deep breaths, trying to stay calm and think what to do. *Is there a 9-1-1 in the Galápagos?* She kind of doubted it, especially from a ship out in a remote part of the islands. *What about the people on shore? Are these goons pirates? Are they going to steal stuff and leave? Or maybe they're going to take the ship and leave the people on the island, including Luke and Dad.* Ezzy suddenly wished she were on the island surrounded by lots and lots of wild animals.

Ezzy sat for what seemed a long time trying to come up with a plan or at least the courage to leave her hiding spot. She jumped when a loud voice boomed over the ship-wide intercom. "This is the captain speaking. We will be conducting an emergency drill in the next five minutes. All crew and staff report to deck four for your assignments."

With trembling, rubbery legs, Ezzy stood and peeked out the door. The back deck appeared empty. She slipped through the doorway and made her way to the back railing but drew back in a hurry. The other ship was pulling up behind the *Darwin Voyager* and more men stood ready to climb aboard. Things had just gone from bad to worse. Oh, how she missed those booger-sneezing iguanas.

Hijacked!

Ezzy ran back through the crew-only door-way into the small, empty corridor. Should she find a better hiding spot and wait to see what happened, or try to get off the ship? During the emergency drill the first day, the captain had explained that the ship had life rafts that automatically inflated when tossed overboard. She could throw one overboard and then jump for it. But then what? And if she jumped overboard—what about sharks?

Taking a deep breath, Ezzy willed herself to calm down and think. Before doing the abandon ship swim-with-sharks routine, she decided to try to figure out what the men who invaded the ship wanted. If they planned to take the ship and leave everyone on the island, she wanted to be with her dad and brother— even if she had to go overboard and paddle with great whites. Then again, if they were just there to steal stuff, Ezzy hoped they'd leave once they had what they wanted.

As quietly as possible, she crept through the crew corridor to a connecting door and peeked through its small round window. It led to the lounge, behind the bar. Not seeing anyone, she slipped silently through the doorway and crawled behind the bar. Cautiously, she rose to look around. The room was quiet and appeared empty.

Ezzy was about to sneak out from behind the bar when she heard footsteps out on the deck, coming toward the lounge. She hunkered down and curled into a ball in the corner. Finding a dirty towel, Ezzy threw it over her head. It was a ridiculous way to hide, but she didn't have time for anything else. She hoped no one would look behind the bar or worse, want a cold drink.

"This way," someone barked. "Enrique radioed. They're with the crew and captain up on deck four."

The men ran by and soon it was again quiet. Ezzy knew she needed to move. She wanted to move. But her legs didn't seem to agree. Fear held her frozen in place.

Ezzy remained still. She was trembling. Tears threatened. Then she thought of her mother. She remembered how fearless her mom always was. Ezzy balled her fists in determination. Still shaking, she stood up and looked out from behind the bar. It was again silent, with no one in sight. She willed herself to be brave like her mom and crept slowly out into the lounge. A sound, almost like a cough, startled her. She jumped and turned toward the noise.

Sitting on a couch against the wall, where Ezzy couldn't see him before, was the injured guy from the other boat. She padded over and put a finger to her lips, whispering, "They don't know I'm here."

"That's better than me," the man whispered back. "They dumped me here. Guess they figured what can an old guy with a banged-up knee do."

"Do you know who they are?" she asked quietly. "Or what they want? I thought you knew them."

"No, I just met them on the other ship," replied the man. "I don't know what they want. But I can tell you one thing, they're not here for bird-watching."

"We saw an illegal fishing net last night. Maybe it's theirs."

The man shrugged. "Maybe."

"My dad and brother are on the island. Do you think they're going to take the ship and leave them there?"

"I don't know," he said. "But if another ship comes this afternoon to do a hike, they'd find them on the island and notify the authorities."

"But the captain said not many boats come out this way."

"The bigger ones do."

"That's good, I guess."

The door to the deck one level up squeaked as it opened. Garbled voices filtered down.

The man waved Ezzy away. "I think they plan to search the ship. You might want to find a good place to hide."

Ezzy nodded, but she had no idea where to hide. Going behind the bar again was nearly as bad as standing in plain sight, definitely not a good option. Ezzy headed back into the corridor that led from the bar to the stern deck. The narrow space offered little in the way of concealment. She cautiously opened the door to the back deck and peeked out. Off to the side, she noticed a big gray plastic garbage can. It had a raised square lid with a rectangular hole facing out to throw waste in. It didn't look like the best or most comfortable place to hide, but time wasn't on Ezzy's side. She decided, unhappily, that her best bet was to go dumpster diving.

Ezzy ran to the big gray plastic can and quickly removed its cover; inside was a bag about half full of garbage. She pushed the bag aside and climbed in behind it. Then she reached over, grabbed the lid, and wiggled down inside the can. She placed the lid loosely on top. Now squatting with the garbage bag in her lap, Ezzy's head was raised up inside the lid just enough so she could see out its square throw-away hole. The smell inside was horrible and it was hot, very hot. Ezzy adjusted her hips, trying to kneel down, and nearly tipped the thing over. The sound of a door slamming echoed across the deck and two men came into view. Ezzy froze. It was the dark hulky goatee guy and his stringy-haired mustached partner from the other ship.

"Check all the cabins, crew areas, and engine room," mustache man said while caressing his facial hair as if it was a pet. "We'll start loading the gear and take off some of the crew."

"Got it," replied the burly dude. "How long do we have before the people on the island get back?"

"About an hour. So move your big butt."

"That's all muscle pal," he replied flexing his overly large biceps. "Not like your chicken legs and skinny…"

"Just move your pumped-up gluteus," said stringy hair guy, again petting his mustache.

Ezzy rolled her eyes at the conversation, but also breathed a tiny sigh of relief. Based on what they'd said, they weren't going to take the ship and leave the hikers on the island. She wouldn't have to take a swim with the sharks after all.

Soon, a steady stream of men carrying equipment went back and forth across the deck. Ezzy ducked lower. The pail wobbled, and she held her breath, hoping no one would notice. One of the goons with a gun came toward the garbage can and she thought for sure he'd seen it move. She lifted the garbage bag over her head as best as she could. Then she heard a loud spitting sound and felt a thwack on the bag now sitting over her face. Ezzy moaned silently and hoped it was a wad of gum.

She heard more people approaching the deck and peered out cautiously. The first person to appear was the captain. With an angry scowl on his face and wearing just a T-shirt and shorts, the man strode to and down the stairs leading to the stern platform. He was followed by a bunch of similarly dressed crew members and several men with guns.

After what seemed an interminable amount of time, the deck again fell silent. Ezzy's legs and back ached like crazy, she felt soggy with sweat, and she had a pounding headache from the stench. Just as she began to climb out, she heard more voices. People were coming up the stairs from the stern platform. Ezzy sat still and again peered out through the pail's throw-away-hole. It was the returning hikers. She wondered if they knew what was going on.

The stringy hair mustache dude came into view. He was wearing the uniform of an officer on the *Darwin Voyager.* "Right this way, folks. We've got cool drinks for you in the lounge. Lunch will be served uh... soon."

Among the returning guests were Ezzy's father and Luke. Everyone was smiling and chatting. Ezzy wanted to shout to them right there and then, but given the guns the bad guys had, it didn't seem like a great idea. Then she spotted Aiden, and he was headed toward the garbage can. He took aim with an empty plastic water bottle. Ezzy ducked lower and felt another thwack on her head as Aiden said, "Swish!"

"Haven't you heard of *recycling*," she muttered.

Soon it got quiet and the deck was again deserted. As quickly as possible, Ezzy popped off the garbage can's cover and climbed out. *Thank god.* She took a moment to stretch, breathe in some fresh air, and then looked over the railing at the stern. The smaller boat was motoring away.

Sneaking back into the crew corridor, Ezzy nearly ran headfirst into Carlos, the crew member she'd met earlier. "What are you doing back here?" he questioned.

"I know what's going on," she told him.

"Then you'd better pretend like you don't."

"Why'd they take over the ship?"

Carlos shook his head and looked over his shoulder as if someone might be watching. "Don't know, but they're serious. They've got guns." He grabbed a tub and started filling it with ice from a nearby machine. "You'd better go to your cabin or lunch. Just act normal and whatever you do, don't say anything or cause trouble."

"Isn't there something we can do? Someone we can call on a radio or something?"

Carlos stared hard at her. He seemed scared or angry, or maybe both. "No, just do what you're told."

"But..."

"Go, before someone finds you here."

Ezzy hurried into the lounge. It was empty. Even the man with the bandaged knee was gone. She wondered what they'd done with him. He seemed like a

pretty nice guy. She grabbed a glass of water someone had left on the bar (at least she hoped it was
water) and poured it over her head to look even more
sweaty—as if she'd been out hiking—and to hopefully
take away some of the garbage stink. Ezzy walked to
the stairs, trying to stay calm and appear as normal as
possible. On the way down, she almost bumped into
someone coming up. Aiden.

"Hey, snorkel girl! We missed you on the hike. And
it didn't even rain snakes."

"Funny," she replied, trying to skirt around him.

"What happened to you? Why are you all wet?"

"Uh…"

"So, what's with your brother and all the animals?"

Ezzy stopped abruptly. "What do you mean? Did
something happen to Luke?"

"No. I didn't mean anything bad. It's just like… like
the animals are drawn to him or something. Almost as
if he can talk to them."

"My brother can't talk to animals. But he does love
them, all of them, and I think the animals sense that.
It's always been that way." She lowered her voice.
"But look, there's something I need to tell you."

Ezzy was about to tell Aiden about the ship being hijacked when stringy-hair fake officer guy came
up the stairs. He stopped at a glass-covered painting
to look at his reflection and was about to smooth his

mustache when he noticed the two teens. "Hey you, lunch is ready. Better get in there."

"Yeah, okay," Ezzy said, wishing she could tell Aiden what was going on. Instead, she headed down to lunch, but not before looking back at the boy. The mustache man was staring at him.

"Hey dude, what's your problem? I gotta pee and the toilet's over there." Aiden pointed to the men's room.

"Of course," the man said though he continued to stare at the teen suspiciously.

Ezzy hurried into the dining room, hoping that Luke and her father were not out roaming the ship looking for her. Once inside the room, she saw Luke waving from a table.

As she made her way across the dining room, Ezzy tried to be as inconspicuous as possible. She was trying so hard not to be noticed that she bumped into a waiter, who spilled a drink, and then she nearly tripped over one of the selfie twins. "Sorry."

Ezzy joined her family at a table.

"Where were you?" her dad asked. "We checked your cabin and looked around a little, but no Ez."

Ezzy's eyes went wide. "You didn't ask anyone where I was, did you?" She hoped they hadn't said anything to the men that had come aboard. They still didn't know she'd been there when they arrived and knew what was going on.

"No," her father answered with a slightly puzzled look. "We didn't say anything to anyone because we knew pretty quick that sooner or later, you'd show up here, where the food is. Why are you all wet?"

"You missed it, Ez," Luke said speaking super-fast. "We saw a penguin, more boobies, and even a flamingo. It was so close, and the most awesome color ever. Has a neck like a snake. Oops, sorry didn't mean to mention snakes. And then we went to this pond... "

Ezzy held up her hand to stop him, figuring otherwise he'd go on like that forever. She leaned closer. "Dad, while you were..."

"Excuse me," said a man at the adjacent table, interrupting her. "Aren't you the young lady I met earlier?"

It was the injured man and he was sitting at a large table by himself. "Why don't you join me?" he added, staring intently at Ezzy.

Her father turned to him and shrugged. "Sure, why not. C'mon, let's give this gentleman some company."

Ezzy wanted to scream no, but that would definitely draw the attention of the imposter crew. Luke didn't look happy about it either. Her father got up and moved to the other table and gave them the c'mon-kids-move-your-butts look.

Ezzy's father looked at the man curiously. "I don't remember seeing you aboard, but you do look familiar."

Before he could reply, Ezzy jumped in. "Dad, we saw him going the other way on the hike yesterday. But that doesn't matter. I have to tell you something."

"Ezzy, let's be polite," her dad said. "Oh yes, were you with the injured hiker?"

"I am the injured hiker," the man chuckled.

Ezzy squirmed in her chair, wondering why the guy wasn't warning her dad. Telling him what's going on. "Dad, the ship... "

Her father put up his hand to get her to stop talking. "I'm a surgeon. Would you like me to look at your leg?"

"A surgeon? How impressive. It's definitely not that bad. By the way, as I said, I met your lovely daughter earlier. Some of the crew from my ship brought me over to see the doctor while you were out hiking. I think we were the only two left aboard."

Ezzy couldn't figure it out. Why wasn't the guy telling her father what was going on? She leaned closer to her dad. As quietly as possible, yet still loud enough to be heard, she said, "*Dad*, while you were on the island, these guys with guns came on the ship."

Her father looked at her as if she had two heads. "What?"

A little louder she said, "The ship's been invaded, taken over, hijacked!"

Her dad glanced around. "Everything seems pretty normal."

The injured man was now looking at her father with concern.

"My daughter has a very vivid imagination."

Luke pulled on his father's shirt and whispered something to him. Dr. Skylar glanced around again. "Luke here says some of the waiters are new and seem to be acting a bit odd."

As they watched, one waiter dumped an iced tea in Grandma Jones's lap and another seemed to be confused about an order and was having an argument with a passenger.

"Sir," Ezzy said to the man. "You know it's true. Back me up here. Dad, I'm not making this up."

"What's your name, dear?" the man asked.

"Ezzy," she said and then turned to her father and repeated, "A bunch of big goons with guns came on-board while you were on the island."

The injured man just stared at her.

An officer who was overseeing the dining room came by. Ezzy didn't know if he was a real or fake member of the crew. He took note of their empty plates. "Is there a problem here?"

"No, no," said the injured man. "Just having a hard time deciding what to eat. Too many options on the buffet."

"Oh, that happens all the time," the officer said. "Given your leg, sir, if you'd like, I can get you some food."

"Thank you," the man replied.

After the officer left, Ezzy again turned to her father. "I'm not making this up and it's not a joke. Men from another ship took the place of some of the crew."

"Keep your voice down," the injured man finally said. He let out a long sigh and waved them all closer. "Okay, okay. What your daughter says is true. But we need to play along. If we cause a scene, they said someone will get hurt."

"*See*," Ezzy said.

"What do they want?" her father asked nervously.

The man shook his head as the officer returned with a plate loaded with food for him. "The rest of you had better grab something before all the good stuff's gone."

Ezzy wasn't hungry and she didn't think anyone else cared about eating right then. "What should we do?" she asked her father quietly.

"I think this gentleman here is right. We..."

"The name's John, by the way," he interjected.

"We should just play along until we know what this is all about or can find a way to alert the authorities."

"Or like, get the heck off the ship," Ezzy suggested.

Iguana City

After lunch, the Skylar family helped their new friend, John, limp into the lounge. On the way, Ezzy couldn't help but stare at each of the crew members as they passed, wondering which ones were part of the real crew and which ones part of the hijack team.

"Are you sure you're okay here?" Dr. Skylar asked John, who was now settled on a couch with his leg raised. "You could stay with me in my cabin and my son could share his sister's cabin."

"Oh, that's very thoughtful of you. But for now, I'm fine here, and besides I'm expecting to see the ship's doctor soon. We all just need to continue acting normal, so the other passengers don't get wind of what's going on and panic."

"We'll do our best," Dr. Skylar replied. "But if you change your mind on the cabin, let us know. We're in rooms 310 and 312."

They said goodbye and headed to their cabins. Ezzy joined Luke and her dad in their room. Luke immediately slumped onto his bed and turned to his father. "What do they want, dad?"

Now pacing in the narrow space between the beds and a desk, his father shook his head. "I don't know, son."

Ezzy had been rolling that very same question around in her brain for the last several hours. Her father spun on his heel and continued to pace back and forth. It reminded Ezzy of a lion she'd once seen in a cage.

"Did you overhear anything else, Ez?" her father asked. "How many men came aboard?"

Ezzy shook her head. "I'm not sure. But I saw them bring some equipment onboard, these big crates and things. I thought they might be the illegal fishermen whose net we saw last night, but maybe they're smuggling drugs or something."

"But why come on *our* ship?" Luke moaned.

"Cover until they get somewhere to offload the drugs?" she suggested.

Her dad nodded. "Could be, I guess."

"I wish mom was here," Luke moaned.

"Yeah, son," his father said. "Me too. But we've

got each other, and she would want us to be brave, like her."

Luke nodded.

"What should we do?" Ezzy asked.

"I think we should do just what John suggested and pretend that we don't know anything. And Ezzy, that means you need to come on the hike this afternoon."

"Don't worry, dad. I was planning on it. I'll take creepy animals over dangerous thugs with guns any day."

They looked at the daily program, and Dr. Skylar read the afternoon hike description, "Fernandina is the youngest and westernmost of all the islands. It is also one of the most volcanically active islands in the region. The last eruption occurred in June 2018. In 1968, the floor of the caldera sank an amazing 990 feet within a two-week period, and in the early 1970s the coastline was uplifted some nine feet during an earthquake. Today's hike is about a mile and a half long over sand and hardened lava flows. It can be very hot and there may be uneven or slippery spots when walking."

Ezzy turned to her brother. "I talked to the captain earlier and he said they get earthquakes here. And sometimes the earthquakes happen when the volcanoes are about to erupt."

"I think we have other things to worry about right now," her father noted.

"Yeah, but yesterday Luke thought he felt shaking—it could have been an earthquake. Right, Luke?"

Luke nodded. "Yeah, and the animals were acting weird."

"It's possible," their father said. "But look, as I said, I think we have other, much bigger problems to be concerned about right now. Make sure you pack plenty of water for the hike this afternoon and put on lots of sunscreen. Hard to say how long we'll be out there or what's going to happen next."

Luke suddenly stood up and pointed to the desk in the cabin. "Hey, what about the phone? Maybe we can call someone for help."

The phones in the cabin were mainly for calling guest services and other cabins onboard, but they could also make international calls.

Dr. Skylar picked up the phone and put the receiver to his ear. "Nope, not working."

"People will have to notice," Ezzy said. "And then they'll start complaining."

"Yes, and I'm sure whoever these people are, they'll have some excuse. Ez, head to your room and get ready for the hike. And remember, let's not say or do anything to bring undue attention to ourselves or the fact that we know what's going on."

She nodded, but Ezzy wasn't sure how easy that was going to be. Now she had to not freak out at all the way-too-close wild animals *and* pretend that gun-toting goons hadn't taken over the ship. *No problem.*

* * *

About an hour later, as they headed to the stern to disembark for the hike, an announcement came on over the ship-wide intercom. It was Jorge. "Good afternoon ladies and gentlemen, don't... uh... forget to pack water and wear sun protection for this afternoon's hike." His voice sounded a little shaky. "I'd... uh... also like to inform you that... um... some people from the Galápagos National Park will be joining us today to collect samples for scientific studies."

Ezzy thought she heard whispering in the background before Jorge added, "Uh... please stay out of their way and enjoy your hike."

She and Luke looked to their father questioningly.

He shrugged and shook his head.

They hung back as people started loading into a zodiac with Jorge. He and Geovana were quieter than usual and glanced about nervously. Then, seemingly out of nowhere, Aiden appeared in front of Ezzy. "Hey, you coming on the hike?"

"Uh huh."

"Cool. Maybe you can help me film again."

"Whatever," she answered distractedly.

"Is something wrong? You don't look so good."

Her father stepped forward and put his hand on Ezzy's shoulder. "We're fine. Kids might have eaten something bad at lunch. Stomachs are a little upset. I've been trying to get these two to try new things."

Luke and Ezzy rubbed their stomachs as if they weren't feeling well.

"That sucks," Aiden said, looking across the deck to where his parents and sisters stood. "My mom brought a whole bunch of stuff for seasickness, upset stomach, altitude sickness. You name it, we've got it, if you need it."

"No, thanks," Ezzy said. "My dad's a doctor. We're okay. Oh look, they're loading the second boat. Let's go."

"Cool," Aiden said. "We'll be in the same zodiac as you guys. I'll be sure to watch out for snakes."

"Gee, you're just *sooo* funny."

Luke grabbed Ezzy's hand and pulled her to where they got their life jackets before heading onto the stern platform. Stringy-hair mustache guy was helping people into the zodiac. Ezzy avoided eye contact and nearly leapt into the boat. Geovana was already in the zodiac. Her face was drawn and she seemed anxious, fidgeting about in the small space in front of the driver. "Okay, everyone sit down and slide back, cheek-to-cheek."

Soon they were speeding away from the ship. Ezzy turned back to watch as the "crew" loaded a couple of cages onto the other zodiac, which had already dropped off one group of passengers. She tapped her father's arm and nodded toward the stern of the *Darwin Voyager*. The others in the zodiac noticed and turned to watch.

Grandpa Jones looked to Geovana. "Is that the group from the National Park?"

"Looks like it," Geovana replied sullenly.

"What sort of study are they doing?" asked the elderly man, smoothing back his short bright white hair.

"I'm not sure," answered Geovana, before signaling the zodiac driver to speed up and head to the island.

Ezzy stared at the cages and the men dressed like naturalists. Slowly it dawned on her and she knew. She knew what the men were after. They weren't drug smugglers or illegal fishermen. They were poachers. They were going to steal animals. She'd read a story on the Internet about how people try to smuggle the unique wildlife out of the Galápagos and then sell them for big bucks in the exotic animal trade. One guy was arrested at the airport when his duffle bag began wiggling. When she'd read the article, Ezzy couldn't believe people could be that stupid—the man had put live iguanas in his luggage.

She figured the hijackers must be planning on using their ship to smuggle animals out of the Galápagos. Ezzy noticed Luke also staring at the cages and the men loading the other boat. He had probably figured it out too. She hoped he could hold it together. He was just a kid after all, and a totally animal-obsessed kid besides.

About half way to the landing site on Fernandina, Ezzy glanced back at the ship, lamenting over her two, not-good, scary, all around terrible options: gun-toting bad guys on the ship or a wild creature-laden trail. The boat slowed as they neared a small landing pier. Geovana stood up and addressed the group.

"Uh... This is the only landing site on Fernandina. The rest of the island is off limits except for research. As you know, it's the youngest island in the Galápagos. Notice the island's shape, much like an upside-down soup bowl. It is characteristic of the volcanoes here."

Ezzy definitely hadn't been thinking about the shape of the island, not even close. But now that Geovana mentioned it, Fernandina did resemble a colossal green and black striped upside-down soup bowl with a wide rim of black volcanic rocks and short green-leaved mangrove trees.

"How high is it?" asked Aiden's father.

"About 4,800 feet. Okay, we're coming to the landing pier. Watch where it's wet as it can be quite slippery, and please keep an eye out while walking. These are the most productive waters in the Galápagos. Here, deep nutrient-rich ocean water wells up to the surface and creates a very rich marine food web. Because of that, there's a lot of food for the animals here, especially algæ for the marine iguanas. We find the largest marine iguanas in the area and this particular spot has the densest population in the islands."

Oh great, Ezzy thought.

"Sea turtle!" Luke exclaimed, pointing into the clear shallow water beside the boat.

"Look, there's a marine iguana swimming!" Aiden added, pointing to a dark iguana with its limbs plastered against its body and its head sticking up out of the water. The iguana's tail swished back and forth, pushing it forward.

Ezzy looked around. Marine iguanas were everywhere: in the water, climbing out of the water, and lying on the rocks. The place was teeming with the things. She took a deep breath to calm herself. Then a giant black bird swooped past her head, causing her to duck so fast she nearly fell out of the boat.

"Frigatebird," Luke told her. "They like to steal other birds' food."

Geovana gave Luke the thumbs up.

As they approached a small pier, Ezzy noticed sea lions playing in a little rocky pool and a giant gray bird stalking fish nearby. Bright red crabs scuttled over the dark rocks. She looked overhead to see if any hawks were around.

Once beside the small concrete walkway, they climbed out of the boat and took off their lifejackets. Looking down the trail, Ezzy could see a large open flat area surrounded by a forest of mangroves. It was covered with marine iguanas. Not just one or two. Literally, it was a carpet of hideous black booger-sneezing iguanas. Ezzy had grown accustomed to dealing with one or even a few iguanas, but this was on a whole other level. Her father came over and gave his daughter a firm pat on the back, whispering, "They're harmless, Ez. You can do this, no problem."

Luke put his pudgy hand in Ezzy's and led her forward. *Be brave,* Ezzy thought. *Act like you don't want to run away screaming.* She turned back toward the zodiac, but the small boat had already backed away from the landing site so that the next one could pull up. Luke yanked on her hand, pulling her toward the iguana carpet. Aiden was nearby, filming them. *Terrific,* she thought, *he's going to capture my freak-out on camera.* Ahead of her, Grandma and Grandpa Jones used their walking sticks to slowly navigate around the mass of iguanas. Suddenly, a loud crack rang out and before anyone could reach her, Grandma Jones pitched forward. Her walking stick had split in two and she'd done a nosedive right onto the iguana carpet. Eyes wide, Ezzy gasped. *Oh, the horror!*

But then, the most surprising thing happened. Grandma Jones laughed. No blood-curdling scream or shout for help as she went into cardiac arrest, as Ezzy expected. The woman was leaning on one arm and a knee, chuckling. She looked up at the others. "Never thought I'd say this; but thank you iguanas. They broke my fall."

"Oh honey pie, let me help you up," Grandpa Jones said as he helped his wife to her feet. "Are you all right, my darling?"

"Fine, sugar. Just a little fall."

For their part, the iguanas hardly seemed to notice anything had happened. They shuffled silently out of the way, sneezed a bit more, and then simply found another spot to lounge on, one on top of another.

Geovana, Dr. Skylar, and Aiden's father all rushed to the older woman's side.

But Grandma Jones just calmly brushed the dirt off her hands and knees. "I hope I didn't hurt the little dickens. They're actually quite soft."

Ezzy was in shock.

"Any cuts or pains?" Dr. Skylar asked.

"No, really, I'm good and a little tougher than I look." She said, winking at the man. "My walking stick, now that's another story." She looked at the two halves of the aluminum pole. "Oh dear, it's definitely done for."

Geovana took the two pieces of the broken walking stick and shoved them into her backpack. Grandpa Jones tried to give his wife his walking stick, but she waved it away. *She might be old and a little kooky,* Ezzy thought, *but that lady is definitely one tough cookie.* After that, Geovana headed down the trail. Ezzy expected Luke to pull her along, but he hadn't moved. Her brother stood staring at the group of men behind them with a look she'd never seen on him—pure hatred.

Five men had come in the following zodiac. They wore khaki outfits like the naturalists, pretending to be with the Galápagos National Park. Slung across each of their backs was a strange-looking gun.

"C'mon," Ezzy said quietly to Luke. "There's nothing we can do right now. Remember, we're pretending everything's okay."

"They're going to hurt the animals," Luke hissed. He let go of her hand, squatted down, and started chasing the iguanas out of sight.

"Hey! You there! What are you doing?" shouted one of the men. "Stop that. Get going with the rest of the group."

From up ahead, Geovana yelled back, "C'mon, guys."

Dr. Skylar was ahead of them and didn't see when Luke turned and stuck his tongue out at the men behind them. Ezzy stifled a laugh and pulled him forward as they jogged to catch up with the group. Geovana stared at the two of them. She told the others to go ahead, following the sticks marking the trail, and hung back for a moment. "Be careful," she whispered.

Geovana went back to the group and stopped them on what looked like a long slab of black pavement. But it was the strangest looking asphalt Ezzy had ever seen—topped by a series of big twisted ropy-looking wrinkles.

Geovana spread her arms wide. "This is a type of hardened lava called pahoehoe. It's a Hawaiian word and refers to its ropy texture. It forms as rivers, and sheets of flowing lava cool while moving over and around the land. Have any of you ever made chocolate pudding on a stove?"

Given the circumstances, Ezzy thought it was a very odd question.

Grandpa Jones raised his hand. "One of my favorites!"

Grandma Jones smiled, nodded, and added, "It is, especially at Christmas."

Grandpa Jones threw his hands up jokingly. "See, even lava makes her think of Christmas."

Geovana smiled. "Well, this pahoehoe lava forms much like the skin on the surface of chocolate pudding as it begins to cool."

"What?" Aiden said with his GoPro running. "How's that?"

"Once the heat is turned off on the stove, the chocolate pudding begins to cool. At the surface, the pudding in contact with the air begins to cool faster than the pudding below, and a skin starts to form. If you tilt the pan, the surface skin doesn't flow smoothly, but it wrinkles and creates a sort of ropy texture— same with pahoehoe lava. The surface starts cooling and hardening before the lava below it. As the lava flows over and around things, the hardening surface wrinkles and twists to form these ropy looking rocks."

"Excellent analogy, young lady," Grandpa Jones said, smiling.

"Yeah, how about some pahoehoe pudding for dessert," Aiden joked.

Geovana continued, "The other type of lava is much sharper and called aa. Because when you walk over it barefoot you go ah... ah."

Ezzy turned to Luke, thinking that might make him laugh, but he wasn't paying attention. His focus was squarely on the men pretending to be naturalists. They were standing in front of the mangrove trees behind the group. It was the back of a sandy spit that spread out toward the ocean like a big fan. The men had just shot a couple of marine iguanas with red-feathered tranquilizer darts. They were placing the now limp animals into bags for transport to the ship.

Geovana moved ahead, climbing up a long ridge of black pahoehoe lava rock that ran along the side the sandy spit. Aiden and the others followed. Dr. Skylar grabbed Luke's hand and pulled him along. Ezzy trailed after them.

Luke whispered to his father, "Dad, we have to do something. They're hurting the animals and stealing them."

Dr. Skylar squatted down and looked at his son apologetically. "I know son, but right now I'm more worried about you and your sister's safety. There's just not much we can do."

They caught up with the others next to a patch of cactus that resembled golden-colored pudgy fingers covered in spines. Geovana was talking. "This is lava cactus, one of the pioneer plants in the Galápagos. They are one of the very first things that can start growing on the lava rock."

Ezzy winked at Luke. "Now *that* would hurt if you sat on it."

Her brother hardly smiled. His attention was on two men with dart guns pointing to the rocks ahead of the group. Sitting atop the rocks were two skinny brown birds with small ragged wings, along with a penguin. The black and white penguin was only about nine inches tall. Ezzy stared at the penguin. It was so small and so... so cute. Then she realized what an easy shot the penguin would be. Ezzy joined Luke in glaring at the dart-wielding men.

Geovana pointed ahead. "Oh look, there are two flightless cormorants—notice their small, mutated wings and thick, strong legs—and a Galápagos penguin." The naturalist jogged off the lava rock and walked briskly toward the animals. She stopped so that when the group caught up, they were standing between the men with the dart guns and the animals. As she started talking, the men strode purposefully toward the group. Luke glared at them. Suddenly, he jumped up, flapped his arms, began waddling around in a circle and honking loudly—much like a female blue-footed booby. Startled by Luke's noisy antics, the cormorants and penguin hopped down the rocks and dove into the ocean.

Grinning, Luke stopped what he was doing and stood perfectly still. His father shrugged dramatically, shook his head, and said to the group, "Kids, what can you do?"

Ezzy knew that normally Geovana would have said something to Luke about his behavior. Instead, she stood quietly and looked as if she was trying not to smile. Aiden and his sisters stared at Ezzy with raised eyebrows. She tried to think quickly of an excuse for her little brother's strange behavior. "He... uh... really likes to pretend he's one of the animals. Remember the albatross?"

Dr. Skylar leaned down and said loudly to Luke in an overly serious tone, "Son, you know the rules here. We need to keep our distance and be quiet so as not to disturb the animals." Winking, he ruffled his son's hair.

"Okay, dad. Sorry," Luke said, in an equally serious tone.

"Let's keep going," Geovana urged. As she walked, she pointed to the flightless cormorant now in the water nearby. The dark brown bird held its long skinny neck and small head up out of the water and paddled with its wide webbed feet. "Watch closely," she said. "The flightless cormorants are excellent at diving and fishing. When the cormorants first arrived in the Galápagos, they could fly like all the other cormorants in the world. But here in the Galápagos there was so much food for them to eat, like fish and octopus, and so little competition from other birds or animals, that they didn't need to fly between the islands to find a meal. Over time, the cormorants' wings mutated, and they lost the ability to fly. So now they are the world's *only* flightless cormorants."

For the next hour or so, the group hiked around the sandy spit watching sea lions, flightless cormorants, a few penguins, and of course, lots and lots of marine iguanas. The marine iguanas blended in so well with the lava rock, the hikers had to be careful not to step on them.

At first, Ezzy was nervous and jumpy about all the animals. She watched carefully where she walked and made she sure didn't get very close to anything. But, after a while, she realized that even when she got a little closer, the iguanas and other animals hardly noticed her. And she liked watching the penguins. They hopped around on the rocks and dove into the water, where they swam like undersea torpedoes, zooming around. Then they'd pop up like corks. And the white feathers covering their pudgy little bellies gleamed in the sun like freshly fallen snow. Ezzy decided she could watch the penguins for hours without any sort of freak-out. She also liked to see the flightless cormorants dive and then try to figure out where they would come up. She'd seen one come up with a fish that seemed way too big for it to eat. The bird must have tossed the fish into the air and caught it ten times before it found a way to swallow it, which it did in one big gulp. Ezzy was sure the fish would get stuck in the bird's skinny neck. But, amazingly, it went down without a problem.

On the other side of the sandy spit, the group discovered a tiny sea lion pup suckling its mother. Ezzy thought she could even hear it slurping milk. She looked closer. The mother and pup weren't creepy or gross. In fact, the scene was kinda heart-warming. Ezzy stopped and looked around. Was it that the bad guys with guns had distracted her or that compared to them, the animals didn't seem so wild or dangerous anymore? Ezzy wasn't sure why she felt less nervous around the animals, but she was glad. She turned to her father and smiled, pointing to a sea lion posing for photos.

Her father looked at her curiously. Then they both turned to Luke. He was once again doing his blue-footed booby impression, scaring away a few birds and iguanas so that the men couldn't dart them.

During the hike, Ezzy and her father had tried to hide his efforts from the fake naturalists scouting for animals. But they needn't have bothered. It was as if word had spread quickly among the animals, and the poachers were having a hard time catching anything. By the time the group finished the hike and were load-ing into the zodiac, the men looked tired, hot, and very frustrated.

Once back on the stern deck of *the Darwin Voy-ager*, Dr. Skylar pulled Luke and Ezzy aside. He squat-ted so that he was eye level with Luke. "Son, I know you want to help the animals. But I think from now on, we'd better be a little more careful."

Luke just nodded.

The Plan

That night's briefing was torture for Ezzy. All she could do was sit and pretend everything was fine, all the while wondering what was going to happen next and whether, once the bad guys had all the animals they wanted, they would leave. The presentation by the naturalist seemed to go on forever, and then she had to make it through dinner. Nothing looked appetizing. Afterward, she and Luke sat with their father in their cabin.

"So, tomorrow there's a hike and snorkeling in the morning," their father said. "Son, I think you'd better keep your antics to a minimum. The men with guns may not be so nice the second time around. We don't want anyone to get bent out of character or go rental on us."

Luke and Ezzy stared at him.

"Really, dad," Ezzy said. "Even now with the bad sayings."

"Better safe than worried," he added.

Luke smiled.

"Ugh!" Ezzy groaned.

"C'mon, just trying to lighten things up a bit."

"What are they going to do with the animals?" Luke asked.

"What about us?" Ezzy added.

"I'm not sure about the animals," her father answered. "But I think they'll leave once they get what they want."

"But dad," Ezzy said. "Why not just catch the animals in their own boat and take off? Why use our ship?"

"Not sure, Ez. Maybe they figure by tagging along with us, for the most part it looks like a regular tourist cruise in case another ship or someone comes by."

"Do you really think they'll let us go?" she asked.

"I think so. They haven't hurt anyone yet."

"Wish we could do more to help the animals," Luke said sadly. "They could die."

Dr. Skylar turned to his son. "I'm sure the animals will be fine. These guys can't sell them if they are badly hurt or dead. They need to take care of them. But I know how you feel. Luke, I wish we could do more to help, too. However, your safety is my main concern."

For a bit they sat in silence. Luke pouted.

"Hey, there's a movie about the Galápagos being shown in the lounge," Dr. Skylar said. "Maybe that will take our mind off things."

"I don't really feel like it, dad," Ezzy said.

Luke just shook his head.

"No problem," their father replied. "We can stay here and play cards or something."

"No, it's okay. You should go see the movie," Ezzy told him. "We'll stay here and hang out. I'm pretty tired."

"Yeah, you should go," Luke added quickly.

Their father paused and then gave them the "I'm serious" look. "Okay, but I want you two to promise to stay here and not go wandering around the ship. I'll be back soon, and I want you in here or asleep. Got it?"

Ezzy and Luke nodded.

As soon as the door shut, Luke turned to his sister. "We should try to help the animals, Sis."

"Luke, you heard dad. He said to stay here. Besides, he's right, they can't sell dead animals. I'm sure they're okay."

"We should at least look around and see if we can find them."

"We have no idea where they're holding the animals, and those goons have guns, Luke."

"C'mon Sis," Luke pleaded. "Just a look to see if they're okay."

"Luke, if the bad guys don't kill us, dad will."

Luke stared at her with a pathetically pouty face. His chin quivered, and his eyes began to well up. "Please," he begged.

"No."

A tear slid down his cheek. "Please, Sis."

Ezzy hated to see her brother cry. "Luke, c'mon. It's gonna be okay."

"Just a quick look around, pretty please." More tears threatened.

"Okay... just a quick look."

She reluctantly cracked the door and peeked out into the corridor. It was empty. Most of the other passengers were in the lounge watching the movie. Ezzy and Luke tiptoed quietly past the lounge to the stairs and then crept up to the next deck. From there they headed to the stern deck, thinking maybe the animals were near where they were loaded onboard. The deck was empty. When a couple of people came by, Ezzy and Luke pretended to be stargazing. "Oh, look there's the Milky Way," Luke said loudly.

Ezzy nudged her brother with an elbow, whispering, "No need to overdo it."

They reached the stern railing and looked over to see if there was anything on the deck below, but it was too dark to see much. Just then, the stringy haired, mustache dude came up the stairs. Ezzy and Luke went back to fake stargazing. The man seemed to hesitate when he saw them, but then continued on.

"Okay, we've looked around and no animals," Ezzy said. "Let's go back."

In response and before she could grab him, Luke scampered down the stairs to the deck below. Ezzy grunted in frustration and ran after him. The back platform and lower deck area were also empty, and there was still no sign of the animals. Luke pointed to another door with a small round window that had light filtering through. It was labeled "crew only". Ezzy shook her head. Before she could stop him, Luke raced for the door and was through in a flash.

"Crap!" She sprinted after him.

The door led to a brightly lit, narrow corridor. Luke was nowhere in sight. Creeping down the passageway, Ezzy glanced from side to side. She heard a sort of fluttering noise. It seemed to be coming from an open doorway up ahead and to the right. Ezzy tip-toed to the doorway and peeked through. The light in the passageway spilled into the room, illuminating what was inside—a bunch of tightly packed and stacked metal cages and wooden crates with holes in them. Ezzy moved cautiously into the room for a better look. Some of the cages were empty; others had miserable, ragged looking animals inside. And there was Luke, standing beside a small metal cage with a trembling albatross crammed inside. The large bird was sitting with its head and long neck bent awkwardly forward. Its entire body shook and some of its feathers poked out through openings in the cage. Luke had his hand in the cage to stroke the sad-looking albatross as he whispered to it, clearly trying to calm the bird. Next to them was a cage full of marine iguanas, and beside that one containing two blue-footed boobies. One bird appeared to have an injured wing. The room was stifling hot and smelled even worse than sea lion surprise.

"It's awful," Luke cried, tears streaming down his face. "Look how small the cages are, and some of the animals are hurt. We have to help them."

Ezzy knew they should turn and run, get out of there as fast as they could. But Luke was so upset, and it was terrible to see the animals hurt and crammed into the small cages. She hesitated, trying to decide what to do.

"C'mon, Sis," Luke pleaded.

"Okay, okay, let's figure out how to open the cages. But we have to make it quick before anyone comes."

Luke nodded and began working on the cage with the albatross. Ezzy went to the one holding the blue-footed boobies. She found the latch and was just jiggling it when she heard a strange noise, almost like a low growl. Luke popped up from behind the albatross's cage and Ezzy turned toward the sound. A man stood in the doorway silhouetted in the light. His hands were on his hips. "What's going on in here?" he asked.

His face was obscured in shadow, but Ezzy recognized his voice immediately.

"Help us free them," urged Luke. "C'mon, before anyone else comes."

The man strode into the room. A big guy followed

and stood nearby with his legs spread wide and a look on his face that suggested he might enjoy a late-night two-kid snack.

Ezzy turned to her brother. "I don't think he wants to help us free the animals."

"Why not?" Luke said. "C'mon, help us."

"I knew you were trouble," the man snapped. "The two of you. I heard what went on, on the island. Little Master Luke's games to scare away the animals."

Luke still seemed confused.

"Luke," Ezzy said. "He's one of them. One of the bad guys."

The man bristled. "Not one of them. These are my men."

"What?" Luke said. "Why? Why are you doing this?"

"Why do you think?"

Ezzy stared hard at the man whose leg seemed to have healed miraculously. "Money. It's all about money. You're going to sell the animals to the highest bidder."

"Oh, my dear, nothing as pedestrian as that. This is the Galápagos. Many of these animals are the world's only of their kind. And this place annually draws hundreds of thousands of visitors. Paying visitors."

Luke and Ezzy looked at one another questioningly.

"Think, kids. Didn't you ever see the movie *Jurassic Park*?"

"You're going to create a Galápagos Park somewhere else?" said Ezzy.

"Very good. That's right. With a few animals and their DNA, I can clone them and create my very own private wildlife park unlike anything else in the world. I can even create new hybrid animals, my own Darwinian evolution. It'll be natural selection on my terms. John's own survival of the fittest."

This guy is nuts, Ezzy thought. *Total bonkers.*

"People will pay big bucks to come to my park and not have to deal with all the rules and regulations here. Plus, with climate change, invasive species, and all the other problems humans are bringing to the Galápagos, who knows how long this place will last. I may even be able to genetically create new species that are more resistant to the rising heat and other human-made threats. I'll be doing the world a great favor by conserving these species for future generations. Scientists will applaud my efforts, be awed by my results, and appreciate what I had to do to make it happen. Even if I do have to bend the rules a little."

Ezzy shook her head. "Stealing animals isn't exactly just bending the rules a little."

Luke stared at John. "And you're hurting them. My dad says these animals belong here with the others of their kind."

"Yeah, and nobody will think you're doing the world a great service," Ezzy added. "Geez, what a bunch of baloney. Besides, you're gonna get caught."

"Oh, young lady, don't you think I've thought this through. Española and the other islands were a bonanza of animals all for the taking: albatross, boobies. They are so used to people, it was like stealing candy from a baby. I didn't even realize how easy it would be. With so many animals up for grabs, I needed another, preferably bigger ship. And with all of you onboard, it makes for good cover. After tomorrow's big prize, the capture of a giant tortoise, along with some sea turtle eggs and a few land iguanas, my speedboats will come to ferry us and the animals out to my partner's ship in international waters before anyone can stop us."

"What about us and all the people on the ship?" Ezzy asked nervously, not sure she wanted to know the answer.

"Once we're gone, you're on your own."

Ezzy stared at him suspiciously. Was he telling the truth? Were they going to just leave the ship and not hurt anyone?

"C'mon," John said. "I think it's time we go and have a little chat with your father. What was it? Cabins 310 and 312?"

The man's goon followed behind and marched them out of the room. Ezzy knew they were in deep doo-doo, in so many ways. This guy John wouldn't have to kill them; their father would take care of that for him.

A Bad Bedtime Story

Using a master card key, John opened the cabin door and led Ezzy and Luke inside. The other passengers were still in the lounge watching the movie.

"Sit," he ordered.

Sitting on the bed with her brother, Ezzy grabbed Luke's hand and held it tight. She stared at John, and her anger grew. She was so mad it overshadowed her fear. She didn't even realize she was squeezing Luke's hand tighter and tighter, until he nudged her and said, "Ouch."

She released her grip. "Sorry."

They sat in silence. Luke was near to tears. Ezzy was tense and continued to glare angrily at John. Soon they heard someone swipe a card key to unlock the door. Seconds later, Dr. Skylar strode into the room. At first, he saw only his kids sitting on the bed. "What's wrong? Why are you two still up?"

Then he noticed the others in the room. "John, what are you doing here? And who's this guy?"

"Have a seat," John ordered.

Clearly puzzled, Dr. Skylar sat on the other bed.

John smoothed his now slicked-back hair. He had on a pink polo shirt and neatly pressed khaki pants. "I had hoped to keep this all quite civilized. But as soon as I met your daughter, I should have known she was trouble. I even told her to go hide as a test to see if my men could find her." He nodded to his crusty associate. "Hard to get good help out here." The other man scowled.

"What's this all about? Why are you in my cabin?"

"You invited me, remember?" John replied arrogantly. "But more to the point. Your two little darlings here have been snooping around the ship and I don't like it. I found them in with my animals who, by the way, need their rest for the long journey ahead."

"What?" Dr. Skylar said, staring at his kids. He then turned back to John. "Your animals?"

"Now, here's what's going to happen next. Either you all cooperate, or you'll be locked in here due to an unexplained and quite possibly fatal injury. I assume you'll choose the former option. So tonight, you will stay in your cabins and get a good night's rest."

"Ha," Ezzy blurted out.

"And tomorrow, you're going to pretend everything is fine. You'll go out on the hike and snorkel in the morning and enjoy all the wonders of the Galápagos. After that, we'll leave the ship and be out of your way. But if there's any more bad behavior, snooping, or scaring the animals off, things will not be so pleasant."

John headed for the door, then paused, turning back. "Just remembered. You're a doctor, aren't you?"

"Surgeon."

"In that case, I could use your help with some of the animals we've already collected. I'm afraid they've gotten a bit banged up. Unfortunately, my men are not the most gentle. The ship's doctor could use some help. Dr.? I'm sorry I haven't gotten your name."

"Skylar. Dr. Skylar."

"Well, Dr. Skylar, tomorrow morning you'll be staying on the ship to help with the animals while your two lovely children here go for a hike."

"I'm not a veterinarian."

"Close enough. Besides, having you onboard with me might help keep these two clowns in line. Wouldn't want anything to happen to daddy, now would we?"

Ezzy wanted to jump up and strangle the man.

Her father must have known what she was thinking as he put a firm hand on her leg.

"I'll let Geovana know that you kids will be going

out with her in the morning and that your father here will be staying aboard. Now sleep tight and don't let the bed bugs bite." With a cackling laugh he left, shutting the door.

For a moment they sat in stunned silence. Then Dr. Skylar turned to Ezzy and Luke. "What's this about you two snooping around the ship?"

Ezzy had hoped he'd forgotten about that. "C'mon, dad. We've got bigger problems." She then told him what John said in the storage room about his plans. "Do you think he's really going to leave once they have all the animals they want?"

"First off," he said. "I thought I told you two to sit tight?"

Luke stared at the floor like a dog with its tail between its legs.

Looking directly at Ezzy, Dr. Skylar added, "You're the oldest, Esmeralda. You should know better."

"Yeah dad. I know. I screwed up and I'm really sorry. But what do you think this guy's going to do with us?"

Staring at Luke, he hesitated before saying, "Hopefully, just as he said. They'll leave once they have all the animals he wants. Okay, Luke, you get ready for bed and tomorrow I want you to behave and do everything Ezzy tells you to."

Luke nodded.

"Ezzy, come on, let's get you into your cabin and to bed as well."

Ezzy hugged Luke tightly, whispering. "It's gonna be okay." She wanted to believe it.

Her father led her into the other cabin. He sat on one of the beds and stared at her.

"I know, I know," Ezzy said. "I messed up."

"I know you know, Ezzy. That's not what I want to talk to you about." He patted the bed next to him and she sat down. "It's about tomorrow. I don't really think this guy is going to just leave with his animals. I said that for Luke. I doubt the man's going to want to leave behind a ship full of witnesses."

She nodded nervously.

"Tomorrow, I want you to talk to Geovana. I want you to find a place for you and Luke to either hide in or run away to. If Geovana and the others want to go with you, that's fine. But what's more important is that you *do not* come back to this ship."

"But dad, what about you?"

"I'll be fine. I'll find a way to get off the ship. I'm a strong swimmer. If we can find a place to wait until another ship comes by, we'll be fine. I'll give you my backpack in the morning and we'll pack as much as we can in it. Ask Geovana if there's another landing site nearby and if you can, go there."

Her voice quivered. "We can't just leave you here."

"You have to, honey. And you're going to have to be brave and set an example for Luke. Don't tell him until you have to."

A big lump formed in Ezzy's throat. She nodded.

"You can do this. Just remember, whatever happens, *do not* come back to this ship. I'll jump off and swim in. Maybe you can leave a message somehow to let me know where you are."

"Okay," she muttered.

Her father then hugged Ezzy super tight. "I love you, Ez, and your mom would be so proud of you. I know you can do this. You just have to believe it yourself."

"I love you too, dad," said Ezzy, trying hard not to cry. "You have to make it to shore. Luke needs you. I need you."

After another long hug, her father left to go sleep with Luke in their cabin. Ezzy lay in bed thinking she'd never fall asleep. She was scared and wasn't sure she could do what her father was asking of her. Then she thought about the men on the ship, her family, and the animals being hurt and kidnapped. Soon her fear turned back to anger—and then, determination. She couldn't let John hurt her family. She had to be brave, just like her father said and like her mother. She had to do whatever it took to keep Luke safe and to meet up with her dad—even if it meant hugging iguanas or swimming with sharks. And maybe, just maybe she could also find someway to stop John and ruin his nutcase plan.

At some point Ezzy must have dozed off, because the phone in the cabin started ringing and woke her up. She reached over and grabbed it. "Time to wake up for another wonderful day here in the Galápagos." It was John. She hung up as fast as she could. "Jerk!"

Isabela Awakens

reakfast began as a quiet affair. Ezzy didn't feel like talking and still wasn't very hungry. Then she thought of what lay ahead and knew she had to eat. She also had to set an example for Luke who was sitting beside her, picking gloomily at his food. Ezzy smothered a piece of toast with gobs of grape jelly and took a bite. She then ate some scrambled eggs and nudged her brother. "Eat something, Luke."

"She's right," her father added. "You'll need energy for the morning's hike."

Luke grimaced, but ate some cereal.

A little later, while Ezzy was getting ready for the morning excursion, her father brought her his backpack and explained what was in it. When she was all set to go, Ezzy knocked on the other cabin to see if Luke was ready.

Dr. Skylar walked his two kids toward the stern. In the lounge, Ezzy stopped to look at the wall map of the Galápagos. "Where are we exactly?" she asked.

Her father pulled out the day's program. It also had a map on it. He compared the two and then pointed to the west coast of Isabela, about midway between the northern and southern tips of the island. "This morning's hike is here, at Urbina Bay."

Ezzy remembered the captain saying there was a village on the island. She thought back to its location, but unfortunately the spot was far from Urbina Bay. She looked for another landing site nearby. If there was one, it wasn't shown on the map.

Once on the stern deck, her father wrapped Ezzy in his arms. He bent down and drew Luke in close. "Son, I want you to do everything Ezzy tells you to. Okay?"

"Yes, dad."

"I know this is scary, but everything is going to be okay. I'll help John with the animals and then see you later."

"Maybe I can stay here with you?" Luke said, choking up.

He smiled warmly. "No, son. I need you to look after your sister. You know how she is with animals and all."

Luke nodded.

"Yeah, I need you buddy," Ezzy told him. "We'll see dad in no time." *I hope.*

"Okay, one more hug and off you go," their father said. "I love you both very much." Ezzy could tell he was working hard to hold it together.

She grabbed Luke's hand and squeezed it as they headed down the stairs. Geovana was waiting for them with two lifejackets. She led Ezzy and Luke into the first zodiac leaving the ship. The usual cast of characters were already aboard including the elderly Joneses and Aiden with his family.

"Where's your father?" Aiden's dad asked.

Ezzy tried to think of an explanation for why he wasn't there. "Um..."

Geovana jumped in. "Dr. Skylar sprained his ankle yesterday and is staying aboard to rest it."

"Oh, what a shame," Aiden's mother commented.

You're telling me, Ezzy thought.

Just before they pushed back from the ship, one of John's men, dressed as a naturalist, jumped aboard. He had a dart gun and pack slung over his back. He nodded to Geovana and then stared directly at Ezzy and grinned.

Uh oh. Not good.

It was another warm, muggy day in the Galápagos. The seas were a little choppy and some puffy clouds hovered over the island of Isabela. They headed toward shore. Ezzy looked back at the *Darwin Voyager*, wondering if she'd ever see the ship or her father again. Then she turned to Luke. He looked so small, sad, and vulnerable. It was all so unfair. He'd already lost his mother and now this. Her anger bristled. Her father was a good swimmer and super smart, he'd find a way to get off the ship. Ezzy's job was to keep Luke safe. She had to do whatever it took to protect her little brother and get back together with her dad.

Ezzy studied the island. The coast stretched for as far as she could see, both right and left. Dark scraggly volcanic rocks lined the shore. In some places sand had accumulated between the rocks, creating small beaches. Behind the shore, the island rose to a high ridge blanketed by shrubs and small trees. In the distance were the silhouettes of several high volcanoes.

The zodiac began to slow as they approached a small black sand beach nestled between rocky outcroppings. It was a wet landing, meaning they had to take off their shoes and jump off the zodiac into shallow water.

The bad guy dressed as a naturalist jumped off first and stood on the beach watching as they disembarked. Ezzy moved forward as Luke went to the bow and swung his legs out of the boat. Geovana helped him jump off. Ezzy handed her the mesh bag with their snorkeling gear and followed. Directed by Geovana, the group headed to the dry sand and scattered dark rocks on the far-left side of the beach. While everyone dried their feet and put on hiking shoes, Geovana collected the lifejackets. As Ezzy handed hers over, she whispered, "I need to talk to you for a minute. It's important."

Geovana glanced at the man with the dart gun. His gaze was laser focused on the two of them. "Not now," she replied. "Okay, everyone ready to go? Leave your snorkeling gear here on the beach."

With a small towel from her backpack, Ezzy quickly dried off her feet and put on her hiking sandals. She nudged Luke to do the same. He had been staring at a second group of men who had landed and were arranging their collecting gear.

A few minutes later, Geovana led the group to a packed dirt trail behind the beach. She stopped and directed their attention to the green bushes beside the path. "Take care with these plants, they have nasty spines."

Ezzy pulled her brother forward. "C'mon, Luke. Let's go." Right behind them was John's goon. Clearly the guy had been told to watch them.

The vegetation grew thick around the trail. As they walked, small birds flitted about in the surrounding tall grass, trees, and spiny bushes. The group soon stopped at a small, open, circular area.

Geovana pointed to a wide leafy tree with a base that split into several thin trunks. Tiny green apples hung from its branches. "This is a manchineel tree, also known as poison apple. The tree's sap will cause a severe rash, so stay out from under it, and the apples are poisonous. Though the giant tortoises love them." She scanned the area and pointed to a small low tunnel carved into the underbrush. "That's the trail of a giant tortoise. Keep an eye out for them. They resemble large dark brown boulders. Also watch your step on the trail. The giant tortoises like to use the trails to get around and they leave exceptionally large droppings behind."

Ezzy thought about the tortoise poop and the poison apple tree. She wondered if fake naturalist guy behind them was hungry. *How about a little apple snack?* She didn't think he'd actually fall for the old wicked witch poison apple trick, but it was a pleasing thought.

They continued down the trail. Most everyone in the group was peering into the underbrush, looking for giant tortoises. Ezzy was busy trying to figure out when and how she was going to explain things to Luke. And then, how they were going to avoid going back to the ship. She was so distracted, she almost stepped on a giant fibrous tortoise turd; at least that's what Ezzy assumed it was. When the group stopped up ahead, she nearly plowed into Luke. "Sorry."

"Large land iguana in the trail ahead," Geovana announced. "Please walk quietly around it. They can be quite skittish. Notice how its color and shape differ from the marine iguanas. You'll also see numerous large holes in the dirt along the trail; those are their burrows. They each have a specific territory within the area."

People stopped to take photographs and then walked carefully around the iguana. Aiden squatted down and filmed with his GoPro. When it was Luke's turn, he hung back waiting for Ezzy to go ahead of him. She didn't move. The land iguana was bright yellowish orange, over two feet long with a big head, thick scaly skin, long tail, and muscular legs. Luke gave his sister a friendly shove. She still didn't budge. "C'mon Sis, they're cool."

"You go first."

"No, Ez," Luke said surprisingly strongly. "You go."

She turned to him and shook her head. Ezzy was less nervous about walking around the large iguana than before, but still it wasn't easy for her. She also wondered if Luke was planning on doing something. Lately her shy little brother had become an all-too-daring wildlife warrior. The man behind them must have thought the same thing. "Get going."

Ezzy crept cautiously forward, skirting around the iguana draped across the trail. Its beady eyes seemed to follow her, and out of its mouth slithered a pink forked tongue. *Okay that was creepy*, she thought. Then Luke stepped forward. A stone sticking up in the trail seemed to catch his toe and he tumbled down, landing with a thump right beside the iguana. It reacted instantly, scampering into the bushes.

The big guy at the back swung his dart gun around. From the ground, Luke turned to him and shrugged. "Sorry, I tripped."

Ezzy quickly helped Luke up and they ran forward to catch up with the others. "Luke, what are you doing?" she whispered.

"Sis, I tripped, really."

"Uh huh."

On the trail ahead, the group had again stopped. Geovana was talking. "This is a female, probably about seventy years old."

Luke and Ezzy joined the group and looked to see what the naturalist was referring to. In the middle of the path, lumbering toward them, was a big dark brown giant tortoise. Ezzy now understood why people mistook them for boulders. The giant tortoise's domed shell must have been three feet wide and it stood over two feet tall. It had short, thick, leathery legs, a small head, and a surprisingly long, skinny neck. What Ezzy found most surprising was just how wrinkly its tan face and neck were—they looked ancient and in serious need of some heavy-duty anti-aging cream.

"Okay, take a photo and then quietly walk around."

Each person silently approached the giant tortoise and then passed by. Aiden squatted down to get a shot of the tortoise's aged face. Unexpectedly and with surprising speed, the animal extended its long skinny neck and head out toward him. Startled, he fell back onto his butt.

It was a much-needed moment of humor, and Ezzy couldn't help but snicker. Even Luke giggled.

Aiden stood up, wiping the dirt off his shorts. "Ha, ha."

Luke stopped in front of the tortoise, and the guy behind said, "Don't even think about it."

Ezzy couldn't imagine what the guy thought was going to happen. The giant tortoise wasn't about to run away any time soon, no matter what her brother did. It probably weighed a ton, and when it moved, it was slower than molasses. Her dad probably would've said something like slower than Kool-Aid. Thinking of her father brought a wave of emotion. Ezzy's anger and determination blossomed back to life. She clenched her fists and stared angrily at John's thug.

Luke watched the giant tortoise and then closed his eyes as if willing it to somehow run away. He made his way slowly around it. Ezzy followed. The man behind them pulled a small radio from his pocket. "There's one of them turtles in the trail up ahead." He paused, staring at Ezzy and Luke. "Nothing I can't handle."

"It's a tortoise," Luke snarled. "Not a turtle."

The trail snaked through a forest of green-leaved skinny trees. Soon they came to an open grassy field. Geovana stopped and pointed to numerous large brown humps in the grass. "The giant tortoises will stay down here this time of year and feed. During the cool season, they'll go up to the highlands. Let's take a water break before moving on."

Pulling a bottle of water from her backpack, Ezzy handed it to Luke. "Hang here for a minute, I need to talk to Geovana." She hoped the big guy wouldn't follow her, but of course he did. It looked like she wasn't going to get a chance to talk to the naturalist in private. She still needed to speak with Luke alone. She spotted the elderly Joneses and had an idea.

"Geovana," Ezzy said loud enough for the bad guy to hear. "Uh... Luke needs to go, if you know what I mean."

Luke stared at her curiously. She gave him what she hoped was a just-go-along-with-me look.

Geovana pointed to a cluster of bushes at the edge of the field. "He can go behind there if he needs to, but don't go far."

Ezzy walked back to her brother and whispered, "Come with me, and pretend you need to pee."

Luke crossed his legs and waddled around as they headed to the bushes. John's henchman started to follow.

"Hey pal, bathroom break," Ezzy said sharply. "Give us a little space, would ya."

The guy eyed them like he was deciding what to do. "Make it quick."

Ezzy guided Luke behind the bushes. "We need to talk. Don't say anything, just listen." As quickly and as calmly as she could, Ezzy explained what their father had told her to do and that he planned to jump off the ship. Luke stayed silent and stared at his sister. "He said, no matter what, we shouldn't go back to the ship."

"Dad's going to jump off the ship?"

She nodded.

"What about everyone else? And the animals?"

"I know, Luke. I want to help them too, but right now it's you I'm worried about."

"Where are we going to go or hide?"

"I don't know yet, but keep your eyes open and be ready to run if I say so."

Luke nodded. Ezzy hugged him. "We can do this, buddy."

"Hey, what's going on back there?" yelled the man.

They walked out from behind the bushes and Ezzy said, "Geez, can't a kid have a little privacy."

By now the other passengers in the group knew something was up and that the man with them wasn't just another naturalist with the Park. Aiden stared questioningly at Ezzy, and Grandma Jones asked, "Is everything okay, kids?"

"Yeah, we're okay," she replied. Then as innocently as a possible, Ezzy turned to Geovana. "Hey, are there any other visitor sites near here?"

The naturalist paused. "I'd say the closest is Tagus Cove to the north. By water, it's not that far."

As she spoke, a rustling in the trees drew everyone's attention. A flurry of small birds flew out and took to the sky. From the bushes came a scuttling sound. Two large land iguanas scampered across the trail ahead.

"What's going on?" Aiden asked, readying his camera.

An instant later the ground began to tremble, and a far-off deep rumbling sound echoed across the island.

"What's that?" one of the selfie twins asked.

"Earthquake," offered Ezzy.

The shaking stopped and Geovana glanced nervously toward the island's interior. "It's just a small earthquake. Happens sometimes around here. I'm sure it's nothing to worry about."

Ezzy thought about what the captain had told her. "What about the volcanoes? Could one be about to erupt?"

"I..."

Before Geovana could answer, another earthquake hit. This time the ground shook more violently. Grandpa Jones grabbed his wife. The selfie twins dropped their phones. And Aiden hit the start button on his GoPro. Ezzy held onto Luke.

Once the ground was again still, Geovana reached into her pocket where she usually carried her radio. It was empty now. She muttered something under her breath, before saying, "Okay, I think we'd better head back to the beach. Follow me."

The group turned around and headed back the

way they'd come. John's thug was the first to go. Ezzy and Luke purposely lagged behind and quickly lost sight of the group. Geovana came jogging back. "Everything okay here?"

"We don't want to go back to the ship," Ezzy told her. "My dad thinks these guys aren't going to just leave us all nice and happy when they've got their animals."

"What does he think they're going to do?"

Ezzy didn't want to spell it out for the naturalist with Luke right there. "I'm not sure. But my dad's going to jump off the ship and swim in. He told us to hide or go to another landing site if we can. How far is that other place you mentioned?"

"Tagus Cove. It's not far by ship, but I've never hiked there from here. I don't even know if there are any trails that way. What about the others?"

Ezzy shook her head. "I don't know. What can we do?"

The ground again trembled.

"Yo! You back there," a deep voice shouted. "Get moving."

They walked slowly toward the beach. Ezzy looked around desperately for a place to hide, but the vegetation around them was thick and impenetrable. The animals they'd seen before were gone.

At the beach, things had changed and not for the better. People were huddled in small groups, while two men loaded a sleeping land iguana and giant tortoise into a zodiac. Three other men, including their goon hiking buddy, watched over the groups, dart guns at the ready. One of the preppy golf guys who'd hiked with them the day before lay on the ground. It looked like he'd been darted. His buddy sat nearby, trying to wake him.

The burly hijacker with the goatee had his dart gun trained on the group. "Guess the gig is up. No, we're not from the National Park, but we're still going to take these animals. The sedative in the darts is made for them, but it will also knock you out. If you're lucky, you'll survive. But I wouldn't test it."

Aiden was standing next to Ezzy. "You knew, didn't you?"

She nodded. "They're holding my dad on the ship. He told us not to go back there, but to find a place to hide or run away." Shaking her head, she added, "But *dang*, I think it may be too late for that now."

Aiden stared angrily at the men with the guns. He then quietly palmed his small GoPro and flicked it on with his thumb. He inconspicuously aimed it at the poachers. The ground trembled again and a radio in the goatee guy's other hand squawked, "Go team one, come in."

Eyeing the crowd, the man put the radio to his ear. "Go team one, over."

Ezzy couldn't hear what was being said, but the man hardly blinked. "Roger that."

By now the elderly Joneses were hugging and whispering to one another. Ezzy hoped one of them wasn't going to faint or worse. Aiden's father, mother, and twin sisters were huddled together. Geovana and Jorge stood with the other passengers.

"Well, folks," said goatee goon. "Slight change in plans. Seems there's a little smoke coming from one of the nearby volcanoes and it might bring some unwanted attention to the area. They'll be no time for snorkeling." He snickered before continuing, "Instead, it'll be a quick trip back to the ship for all of you." He paused. "Well, except maybe you two ragamuffins." He pointed his gun at Luke and Ezzy. As he turned toward them, he stopped and stared at Aiden. "What the...?"

In several long swift powerful strides, the man was standing in front of Aiden. "Not smart, kid. Hand over the camera. We're going to collect them all later anyway, but I'll take yours now."

Aiden didn't move.

"Son, do as the man says," his father urged.

Aiden reached forward like he was going to give the guy the camera, but instead he opened his hand and let it fall to the sand. "Oops."

The man scowled and muttered, "*Kids.*" As he reached down to pick up the camera, Aiden lunged forward, tackling him. At the same time, he turned his head toward Ezzy and shouted, "Run!"

Tortoise Tunnels

There was no time to think. Ezzy grabbed Luke's hand and sprinted for the trail.

"Get them!" shouted the man on the ground.

Their move to escape was so unexpected, the men were slow to react. It gave them a head start—Ezzy hoped it would be enough. She whipped by an over-hanging spiny branch and felt it slash her shoulder. She kept running, pulling Luke along. The trail was flat and easy to follow, but still Ezzy knew they couldn't outrun John's men. They needed a place to hide, and fast. Then Luke skidded to a stop, yanking on her hand, and pulling her to a halt.

"There!" He pointed to the giant tortoise trail that Geovana had shown them earlier. It was a small dark tunnel cut into the thick vegetation lining the trail. She knew exactly what he was thinking. "You go first."

Luke dove in and scurried into the tunnel. Ezzy followed, praying she'd fit. With the backpack on, it was a tight squeeze. Branches scraped her legs and arms. Still, she crawled ahead. It got darker. She caught up to Luke and grabbed his foot, whispering, "Stop and sit still. Don't make a sound."

Ezzy reached back and fluffed up some dead leaves in the tunnel to cover their trail. Seconds later she heard footsteps pound by on the path. They held their breath and stayed on their hands and knees. It was hot and stuffy in the tortoise tunnel, and Ezzy was sure she was kneeling on a giant tortoise turd. Eventually, after what seemed like a really long time, but was probably only a few minutes, she heard the men come back and pass by.

After that, they waited for as long as they could stand it before crawling out of the tunnel. Ezzy greedily breathed in the fresh air and scraped the tortoise poop off her knees. *Yuck!*

Luke turned back toward the beach. "Can we maybe go back and see what's going on?"

Ezzy wanted to go back, but then again, she didn't. Truthfully, she wasn't sure what to do or where to go. Curiosity, indecision, and Luke won out, and they crept cautiously back to where the trail opened up onto the beach. They crouched behind some bushes and peeked out.

The beach appeared empty, and in the distance a pair of zodiacs were motoring away, back toward the ship. That was a relief. Then Ezzy caught sight of Aiden. He was sitting on the sand where he'd tackled one of John's men. He had his hand pressed to his leg and looked a little woozy.

Ezzy ran over to him. "Aiden, what happened? Why are you still here?"

Luke joined them and pulled a water bottle from his small backpack and handed it to him.

"Thanks," Aiden said taking a gulp. "When I jumped that guy, he got a shot off and it nicked my leg. Guess I was lucky, I didn't get a full dose of whatever's in those darts." He raised his hand. Blood seeped out of a raw red gash across his thigh just below his shorts.

Taking off her backpack, Ezzy removed her dad's first aid kit. "Here, let me help. Why'd they leave you here?"

As she cleaned and bandaged the wound, Aiden explained what had happened, "After you two left..."

"Thanks, by the way," Ezzy said.

"Yeah," Luke added.

"If something bad was going to happen, I figured at least you two might get away. Anyway, after you guys hightailed it outta here and I'd been shot at, everyone else was too scared to say or do anything. Geovana and Jorge tried to keep everyone calm. I don't think they wanted anyone else to get hurt. Those men just about threw that one unconscious guy into the zodiac. Then they loaded everyone else into the boats to take them back to the ship."

"How come they left you here?" Ezzy repeated.

"They said they wanted to teach me a lesson and that they planned to send a team back to find you two and that I'd be collected then. So, what's going on? Who are these guys?"

As Ezzy started to explain the ground again shook and they heard more rumbling in the distance.

"That can't be good," Aiden said.

Then Luke pointed toward the *Darwin Voyager*. "Look!"

Two zodiacs were racing back toward the beach. "Uh oh," Ezzy said. "That's definitely not good." She turned to Aiden. "Can you run?"

He stood up and tried his leg. "I think so, but where? What about the others and my family?"

"I've been thinking about that. I think our best bet is to go to the other landing site Geovana told us about and try to flag down another ship. They can radio the Park, local police or whoever to get help."

"What about dad?" Luke asked.

"We'll leave him a message." She didn't want to add in front of Luke—if he makes it off the ship.

"How?" Luke said. "With what?"

Ezzy hadn't quite figured that part out or how they were going to get to Tagus Cove.

Aiden limped over to a big black rock to their left. "Before Geovana left, I saw her doing something over here. Maybe she was leaving some supplies or something."

Ezzy and Luke followed him around the rock. It was about the size of a big gravestone with a jagged top and wide base.

"She's one smart cookie," Aiden said staring at the backside of the rock.

On a flat section of the dark rock someone had drawn an arrow in what looked like white chalk and below it had written *Tagus*. The arrow pointed along the coast to their right. Sitting on a tiny shelf in the rock was a pencil urchin spine like the one Luke had picked up on Española Island.

Luke grabbed the urchin spine and quickly drew a heart. Inside he scratched *4MOM*. "So dad knows it's us."

The zodiacs were getting closer.

"Let's go," Ezzy urged.

Aiden looked unsure.

"Do you have a better idea?"

He shook his head. They took off on the soft sand following the arrow. Aiden limped along doing his best to keep up. They were headed toward a stack of dark volcanic boulders at the far end of the beach.

Ezzy ran. She didn't think or worry about avoiding any animals or their poop. They were the least of her concerns now. She needed to get away from John's thugs and find help as fast as possible.

At the end of the beach, they stopped to catch their breath and see where the men from the ship were. John's minions had just landed on the beach and were busy disembarking from a zodiac.

Ezzy stared ahead. Big black boulders blocked the trail. Waves crashed menacingly on one side of the rocks. On the other was a particularly dense stand of spiny bushes. "We'll have to go over."

She gave Luke a boost up onto the first boulder. He scampered surprisingly easily across it like a little monkey. Ezzy followed less ably and Aiden came up behind her.

"Don't look at my butt," she muttered.

"That's what you're worried about right now?"

"C'mon," Luke said. He was standing up on the rock ahead of them.

Suddenly, a piercingly loud horn rang out. They all jumped. Luke nearly fell off the rocks. Ezzy turned toward the water. A man in one of the zodiacs was pointing at them. Luke scrambled across and off the rocks. Aiden and Ezzy followed as quickly as they could. Ezzy slid off on her butt and Aiden put out his hand to help her across the last boulder. "Thanks."

"No problem, snorkel girl."

Behind the boulders was a steep, sloped, rocky beach that curved around to the right. They raced across the rocks as best they could until Luke suddenly stopped. They were about half way down the beach and out in the open.

"Keep going," Ezzy urged.

But instead of heading along the beach, Luke scampered up the rocks to where the vegetation grew thick and then—he disappeared. Aiden and Ezzy looked at one another and then took off after him. "Luke?" she yelled not too loudly. "Luke?"

At the top of the beach they ran into a thick wall of spiny green bushes and no Luke. Ezzy spotted a thin dirt path that was barely a path at all. It had to be where Luke had gone. Aiden looked at her questioningly. She shrugged and headed for the low narrow cut through the bushes. As she bent over to get through, Ezzy figured Luke had run right under the tangle of spiny branches. Aiden groaned and followed. They did their best to avoid getting scratched. The trail then opened up and there was Luke, standing in the path waiting for them.

"Where are you going?" Ezzy questioned.

He pointed ahead. A large bright orange and yellow land iguana sat perched in the trail as if waiting for them. "I followed it. We can hide better back here."

Ezzy stared ahead, the path seemed to parallel the shore. "The trail looks like it's going in the right direction."

Luke nodded. Then they heard men shouting from the beach behind the bushes.

"Let's get moving," Aiden whispered. "I hope this iguana knows where it's going."

The iguana scurried ahead on the trail and they followed. Luke led the way close behind the creature. The narrow path curved to the left through a thicket of spiny bushes. Ezzy made her way as quickly but as carefully as possible to avoid being stuck. Soon the trail became littered with small white rocks almost like tiny bleached branches or bones. As they crunched under her feet, Ezzy wondered what they were. Around the next turn was an even bigger surprise—one about five feet tall to be exact. It was a white rock resembling a giant mushroom. Further down the path were more of the strangely large mushroom-shaped rocks. It reminded Ezzy of a forest—a weird mutant white mushroom rock forest.

"What's this?" Aiden asked.

Ezzy looked closer. The surface of some of the rocks was made up of tiny pockmarks, others were topped by squiggly grooves.

"I know!" Luke exclaimed. "I read about it."

Of course, Ezzy thought.

"It's an old coral reef. In a book it said there was an earthquake here once and it raised a coral reef up out of the water. There were a lot of dead stinky fish too. That's how they first found it. These are the skeletons of old dead corals."

"No way," Aiden said.

"Yes way," Luke countered.

"It's cool, but we gotta keep moving," Ezzy told them. "Where'd that iguana go?"

Luke scanned the vegetation surrounding the trail. "It must have left. Probably reached the end of its territory."

"How does he know this stuff?" Aiden asked Ezzy.

She shrugged. "When it's about animals or nature, my brother remembers everything he hears or reads. It's kinda freaky."

"Hey!" Luke said.

"Well, which way do we go now?" Aiden asked, staring at the path, which had split into two trails with one veering slightly inland.

Another earthquake shook the ground. It was milder than the last one, but this time it was accompanied by a thunderous rumble.

Ezzy pointed down the inland trail, which headed in the direction of the rumbling. "That way."

"You want to go toward an erupting volcano?" Aiden asked.

"Yup," she answered. "The captain told me that when volcanoes here erupt it draws a lot of attention. And right now, we could use some attention."

"Yeah, but what about the whole lava barbeque thing. Personally, I don't want to be part of the pahoehoe pudding."

"Let's worry about the lava later. Right now, I just want to get away from John's goons and find help."

Aiden agreed, and they set out again, following the trail. It led to an open field of tall grass.

"Hey, look over there," Luke shouted, pointing to a brown hump in the field ahead. "A giant tortoise." He ran toward it.

Aiden and Ezzy jogged after him. "More with the animals?" Aiden questioned.

Ezzy just shrugged.

They caught up to Luke who was standing beside a giant tortoise and pointing to what looked like a line of dark brown boulders. "This way," he told them, heading toward the next giant tortoise in line. It was as if the large creatures were playing a game of follow the leader toward the edge of the field where the last (or first) giant tortoise sat in line. Next to it, the land sloped upward. The group stopped and looked up. The densely vegetated slope rose to a high ridge. It must have been several hundred feet up.

"If we can get up there, maybe we can see the other landing site," Ezzy suggested.

"And the erupting volcano," Aiden added. "But how are we going to get up there?"

Good question, she thought.

Luke got down on his hands and knees and peered in front of the last giant tortoise in line. He pointed ahead. "That's how."

It was another tortoise tunnel and it went up toward the top of the ridge.

"Remember," Luke said. "Geovana said the tortoises go up higher during the cool season."

"See," Ezzy said to Aiden. "He remembers everything. Freaky, but brilliant."

Luke grinned and started crawling. "C'mon!"

"I'm not sure I can fit in there," Aiden said uncertainly.

"Better give it a shot," Ezzy urged. "We may have lost those men on the iguana trail, but when they don't find us, they're going to go back to the ship. After that, they'll leave to meet up with John's speedboats. We need to find help before that happens."

With Luke in hearing range, she didn't want to add *and before they do away with all the witnesses—everyone on that ship.*

Aiden nodded. "Okay, I'll do it. But it isn't going to be pretty."

Luke was already crawling uphill inside the tortoise tunnel. Ezzy went in next. It was hot and dim inside and smelled earthy. A mat of dead and decaying leaves covered the ground. Ezzy tried not to think of all the tortoise turds she was probably crawling on. Aiden entered the tunnel behind her. The branches around her shook and she heard him mutter words she wasn't supposed to use.

Ezzy began crawling up the steep slope. She caught up to Luke and they stopped to wait for Aiden.

He barely fit in the tunnel and was having a tough time making his way through. Once Aiden joined them, the group began crawling upward again. Soon, Ezzy's hands and knees began to throb. "How ya doing up there, buddy?" she asked Luke.

"I'm good, Sis, this is cool."

Cool was definitely not the word Ezzy would use to describe crawling up a steep hill through a stuffy hot tunnel on tortoise poop.

The hill became steeper and their pace slowed to an even slower crawl. Ezzy focused on putting one hand and knee in front of the other. Fortunately, the ground then began to level off. Still, sweat poured into her eyes. Soon, Ezzy realized some of the water dripping down her face was coming from the tangle of branches overhead. And the ground was damp. It was also darker inside the tunnel. In front of her, Luke's pace began to slow even more. "Keep it up, Luke. You'd make a great giant tortoise."

"I think right now I'd rather be a sea lion," he said. "Or even better, a bird."

"I'm with ya, kid," Aiden grunted from behind.

The tunnel floor turned to mushy, leafy mud and got steeper again. Ezzy groaned silently. They started to slip and slide in the mud.

"Now, this is *really* what I call fun," Aiden mumbled.

"It's brighter up ahead," Luke told them.

"Oh please, let that be the top," Ezzy added.

"Amen," Aiden said.

Luke was the first to pop out of the tortoise tunnel. He slid in the mud. Ezzy fell on top of him and Aiden on top of her. They untangled their limbs and pushed themselves up. Streaked with mud and scrapes, they were sitting on a wide shelf-like ledge that ran along the ridge. It was blanketed by grass, large ferns, and a few broad-leaved short trees. Glistening moss hung from the trees' branches, and the ground was slick with moisture. The sun had disappeared behind a shroud of thick gray clouds. It began to drizzle.

"Look," Luke said, shielding his eyes from the light rain and pointing back down the way they'd come. From the top of the ridge, Urbina Bay looked like a bite taken out of the coastline. Two zodiacs were speeding away from the beach toward the *Darwin Voyager.* Ezzy knew it wasn't going to be long before the ship departed. They had to get to Tagus Cove before the ship got too far away. Still, she took a moment to scan the water, looking for any sign of someone swimming toward shore.

"Uh, guys," Aiden said, staring in the exact opposite direction. "I think we have another problem."

Luke and Ezzy turned at the same time. "Whoa," they said in unison.

A mushroom-shaped cloud of light brown ash rose over the steeply sloped volcano in the distance. From a vent on the volcano's side poured orangey-red lava. It flowed like a fiery river downslope. The lava was still pretty far away, but it seemed to be moving toward the coast—exactly where they were headed. It made Ezzy wonder just how fast lava flows.

She turned and looked for the other landing site, but the view was blocked by another ridge, slightly lower than the one they were standing on. "Let's keep going. Hopefully, Tagus Cove is just beyond that next ridge."

"What about the volcano?" Luke asked nervously.

"Yeah, and more importantly, what about the lava?" added Aiden.

As if on cue, the ground shook, and they had to hold onto one another to stay upright. They turned to the erupting mountain in the distance. Like a fiery Las Vegas spectacle, a curtain of glowing orangey-red lava shot into the sky from the vent on the volcano's side.

The Trail Heats Up

Spellbound by the view, Ezzy, Luke, and Aiden watched as a winding river of glowing lava streamed down the side of the volcano.

"It still looks pretty far away," Aiden noted.

Ezzy and Luke nodded nervously.

"C'mon, let's find a way down and over that next ridge," Ezzy urged.

They looked for a way down the back side of the ridge they'd just climbed. The vegetation was less dense, but the slope was steep, covered with loose rocks, and perfect for twisting an ankle or slipping on. Going straight down wasn't an option. Even trying to somehow traverse the hill seemed risky. Luke pointed to the sky. "A hawk."

Ezzy glanced up. A hawk soared high overhead, circling. Still a bit skittish from her last hawk encounter, she ducked behind Aiden. The hawk dove, swooped by them, and landed in a nearby tree. It sat on a branch and seemed to stare right at Luke. The hawk then leapt from its perch and flew away, its talons skimming the top of Luke's head. He didn't even flinch or hesitate—instead he took off, chasing after the bird.

"Luke!" Ezzy yelled.

Aiden gave Ezzy a look suggesting her little brother was a few cards short of a full deck. She printed after the boy, trying not to slip on the wet ground. Aiden followed. Luke scampered along the ridge, his eyes locked on the hawk overhead. He raced toward the far side of the ridge, which appeared to end at a steep cliff.

"Luke, stop!" Ezzy shouted. But he kept going. "Stop!"

Then Luke disappeared—again. Ezzy gasped, not wanting to think the worst. She slid to a stop. Aiden barreled into her. "Sorry."

"Hey, down here!"

Ezzy was relieved to hear Luke's voice and turned quickly to see where he was. Luke was standing on a skinny path that ran in switchbacks down the steep hillside. It wasn't much of a trail, more like a dirt groove through the scattered rocks, but better than nothing. They hurried down as fast as they could.

About mid-way down, Luke stopped abruptly and Ezzy ran into him. Ahead, another creature sat in the trail, but it was unlike anything they'd seen so far.

"What is it?" Ezzy asked.

"Iguana," Luke said, staring at the two-foot-long pink and black striped reptile.

"Yeah, I know it's an iguana, but why's it so... so pink?"

"I read about them," Luke answered. "It's a new species just discovered. It's only found on, like, one volcano."

"I guess this is it," Aiden said from behind.

The iguana eyed Luke and then scurried away. While they were stopped, Ezzy pulled a water bottle from her backpack. She took a sip and passed it around. She still couldn't see what was beyond the ridge ahead. The ash cloud and lava river however, still looked, thankfully, pretty far away.

The slope flattened out and their pace quickened. They were all muddy, cut up, hot, and tired. But they kept going. No one spoke. Ezzy's knees and hands ached from the crawl uphill. But whenever she thought about stopping, she'd think of Luke and her father. *What if he's still on that ship? What about Aiden's family and Grandpa and Grandma Jones, Geovana, and Jorge?* She had to keep going, protect Luke, and help the others. Ezzy steeled herself for whatever lay in the path ahead and then took the lead.

They headed up the second ridge. It was a little less rocky and scattered across the hillside were trees with skinny gray trunks. Ezzy started using the trees as handholds to pull herself up. Luke and Aiden followed her example. Then she remembered what Geovana had said about the poison apple tree's sap being like poison ivy. Ezzy abruptly released her grip, nearly falling over. She leaned in to look closer at the trees' branches. No little green apples. With relief and renewed hope, she grabbed onto a tree and then went from one to another, using them to pull herself up the hillside. Luke and Aiden were right behind her.

Sun peeked out through the clouds. Ezzy's thighs began to ache and each step became a chore. Still, she didn't stop. Ezzy looked back. Luke was struggling. Aiden quickly came alongside him. "It's just a little further. How about a piggyback?"

Ezzy caught Aiden's eye and whispered, "Is your leg okay?"

"Just a scratch. Might feel it later, but for now I'm good. I think moving around really helped."

As Luke got on Aiden's back, Ezzy mouthed a silent thank you. They slogged uphill until finally they reached the crest of the second ridge. Breathing hard, Ezzy peered ahead. And there, just below them, was the coast and a wide semicircular embayment. "That must be Tagus Cove!"

Then Ezzy turned to the volcano. Fountains of glowing molten rock spurted skyward, adding more lava to what now resembled a gigantic red-hot snake curving down the mountainside. It looked like the lava flow might cut off their path to Tagus Cove. Ezzy didn't want to wait to see. She headed downhill as fast as her tired legs could go. Aiden and Luke followed. The other side of the ridge was less steep and soon flattened out. Then another problem arose. The trail was blocked by scraggly bushes and short leafy trees. They had little choice; it was either turn around or bushwhack. *Where's a machete when you need one*, Ezzy thought.

"I'll go first," Aiden offered.

When Ezzy had first met Aiden, she thought he was a jerk—a kinda good-looking jerk, but still a jerk. But now as Luke slid off his back and Aiden got ready to break a path through the bushes for them, she knew she had misjudged him.

"Hold on," Ezzy said, swinging off her backpack and reaching into it. "It might be kinda small for you, but this might help." She gave Aiden her lime green rain jacket. "At least it will help protect your arms." She gave Luke his jacket as well.

"What about you, Sis?" Luke asked.

"I'll go last, it'll be easier."

Aiden stepped forward and began beating back the bushes. He used his arms, legs, and sometimes his entire body. Twigs stuck in his hair, mud lined his face, and soon fresh, thin, bloody scrapes crisscrossed his hands and legs. Luke and Ezzy kept as close behind as possible. They pushed through the low branches and ducked under the higher ones. Every once in a while, a skinny branch whipped back like a spiny spring. It was tough going and slow, and already late in the afternoon. Ezzy encouraged them to move faster. She definitely didn't want to be stuck out there in the dark. Then Aiden stopped.

"What's wrong?" she shouted from behind.

"Come see for yourself."

Ezzy and Luke squeezed forward to peer over Aiden's shoulder.

"Whoa!" said Luke.

Up ahead the vegetation grew much thicker and more dense, but nearly hidden by the overgrowth was the opening to a cave.

"What now?" Aiden questioned.

Ezzy didn't think twice. She headed for the gaping black hole that was the entrance to the cave. "Either we go back or see where this goes."

At the mouth of the cave, Ezzy leaned in to see inside. "Looks pretty big." Maybe the cave was a short cut to the coast. She didn't want to go back, and they couldn't bushwhack through the wall of plants that was the only other way ahead. The new, adventurous Ezzy figured it was worth a shot. She climbed over a few rocks and entered the darkened cavern.

"What's in there, Sis?" Luke shouted.

"Come in," she yelled back. "I think it's a tunnel and looks like it's heading in the right direction." Then Ezzy remembered something else her father had put in the backpack. She searched through it and pulled out what she was looking for.

As Aiden and Luke scrambled into the cave, Ezzy clicked on the small flashlight. The ceiling was at least seven feet high and the tan walls so smooth, they looked as if they'd been carved from the surrounding rock. The floor was flat, almost like pavement.

"Awesome!" Luke exclaimed once inside.

"Nice flashlight," Aiden noted.

"My dad put it in the backpack. Lucky, he's super big on being prepared."

Ezzy aimed the flashlight into the darkness ahead. "I say we give it a go. I don't wanna go back through those bushes again to try to find another way around. This will be much faster." Turning to look at Aiden's scraped hands and legs, she added, "And less painful."

"No argument there," Aiden said. "But what if it's a dead end?"

"What if it's not?" Ezzy offered. "And it's going to be dark soon. This might be our best shot to get help anytime soon."

"But..."

Luke grabbed Aiden's hand. "C'mon. Let's go." He pulled Aiden along as Ezzy led the way into the cave's darkness. She didn't care what sort of animals might be in the cave or about anything else. Ezzy just wanted to get to that cove, find her dad, and get help. They had to maneuver around a few large rocks in the cave, but otherwise it was pretty easy going. They picked up their pace and were soon jogging, guided by the flashlight's narrow beam.

After a while, Ezzy's hands got slippery with sweat. She nearly dropped the flashlight, and the beam wobbled every time she adjusted her grip. Finally, she had to stop to wipe her hands on her shorts. Aiden and Luke stopped with her.

"Sorry, let's keep going," Ezzy said before steadying the flashlight and aiming it ahead. "Crap!"

"Mega-crap!" Aiden added.

Dead ahead was a wall—a wall of rock.

They crept closer. No one said anything. Disappointment hung in the air. Ezzy didn't want to backtrack, but a dead end meant they'd have to. They'd never reach the cove before dark, and what about the lava? Then, as she got closer to the wall, something didn't look right.

"It's another tunnel!" Luke exclaimed, pointing to the left and then right.

He was right; once they got closer, they could see it wasn't a dead end after all. It was the intersection of two tunnels.

Ezzy turned to the left. "The ocean's that way, I think."

Without another word, they headed down the new tunnel. It was a little warmer, so Aiden and Luke took off the rain jackets they'd worn through the bushes. Ezzy stuck the jackets in her backpack. Soon, they were again jogging, hopefully toward the coast and

Tagus Cove. The floor was smoother than before and there weren't any rocks to skirt around. It seemed almost too good to be true. That's until it started to get hot. Not that they'd been in air conditioning before, but suddenly the heat level in the tunnel climbed from bake to broil.

"Ahhh, guys, is it getting hotter in here or what?" Ezzy asked.

Luke, her memory-like-a-steel-trap brother, stopped abruptly and smacked his head with his hand. "Uh oh." He turned slowly around, almost like he didn't want to. Aiden and Ezzy stopped and turned with him.

"What's wrong?" she asked.

"You weren't there the other day," Luke said to her.

"Where?"

"On the hike."

"What hike?"

"The one with the lava tube," Luke answered.

Aiden's eyes grew big. "Dang. You're right."

"What's a lava tube?" Ezzy asked.

Luke glanced around. "Jorge said it's how lava can flow underground from a volcano to the ocean. When the lava stops flowing, it leaves behind big open tubes, *or tunnels*. Kinda like this."

"Uh... does new lava ever flow down old lava tubes?" Ezzy stuttered. "Like, could lava from the erupting volcano flow down this tube?"

No one needed to answer that question, as in addition to the rising heat, a strange orange glow arose in the tunnel behind them.

"Run!" Aiden shouted.

Ezzy didn't need to be told twice—no hands-on lava experience for her. She grabbed Luke's hand and sprinted down the tunnel. Soon the glow from the oncoming lava was so bright, they hardly needed the flashlight. The adrenaline must have kicked in because Ezzy forgot about being tired, her legs aching or anything else. All she could think about was the thousand-degree people-barbecuing lava rushing toward them. They ran for their lives.

Luke started to slow again. Ezzy tugged on his hand to pull him along, but he was clearly exhausted. Aiden tapped her on the shoulder and nodded toward her brother. She let go of Luke's hand and Aiden scooped him up to go piggyback again.

Then, just when Ezzy didn't think it could get any hotter, it did. The lava was catching up. Adrenaline pumped through their veins and they ran harder. The tunnel curved around like a snake and they kept running. Aiden stumbled over some loose rocks. This time it was Ezzy who grabbed his hand and kept him from taking a tumble.

"Thanks!" Aiden said.

"No problem, GoPro man."

Up ahead it started to look a little brighter. As

they got closer, Ezzy could see what looked like the end of the lava tube. *Thank god,* she thought. They were almost there, wherever there was. She didn't really care. Ezzy just wanted out and away from the burning, flowing getting-closer people-frying molten rock. They sprinted for the daylight ahead.

The tunnel ended abruptly... at a steep cliff. Standing at the edge, Ezzy looked down—a long way down. Then she looked back. The river of glowing fiery lava was closing in. No one had to say anything. Ezzy grabbed Luke's hand, and together they jumped. It was at least a two-story drop to the ocean. They landed with a resounding thump and an enormous splash.

Bubbles swarmed around Ezzy as she sank into the blue-green sea. The water was cold, much colder than where they had snorkeled before. But it was also like a slap in the face, and suddenly she felt alert and energized. Ezzy started to kick and pull her way to the surface. Frantically, she looked around for Luke. He popped up nearby, his eyes as wide and round as a baby sea lion's. Aiden broke the surface next, a little off to their left. Together they swam out and away from the lava tube. Once they were a safe distance away, the group stopped, treaded water, and looked back.

Fiery-red lava poured from the rocky tube, streaming into the sea. Where it hit the ocean, the water boiled instantly and thick clouds of steam billowed upward. Glowing molten rock continued to flow out of the tube. It was the lava equivalent of a waterfall—a lavafall.

"Glad you really can swim, snorkel girl," Aiden said, breathing hard while staring at the lava.

"Me too," she said.

"Me three," Luke added.

Then they all spun to scan the water they'd just landed in. There were no ships or even small boats in the surrounding cove. Ezzy started to shiver. They needed to go ashore, but where? Steeply sloping layers of tan and gray rock ringed the cove.

A small yellow head popped up in front of the group. Startled, Ezzy jumped back, bumping into Luke.

"It's a sea turtle, Sis," Luke said, paddling around her.

Ezzy treaded water and watched as the sea turtle lifted its head. She heard an intake of air. The sea turtle turned and began slowly swimming away. Seconds later it stopped, and she could swear it turned back, as if wondering why they didn't follow. Then, something bigger and much faster zoomed by. Ezzy hoped it was Luke or Aiden. But neither had moved. She slowly turned around, praying she wouldn't see a large triangular fin coming their way. Ezzy was feeling brave, but not that brave. Another head popped up just feet away. It was the small whiskered face of a sea lion. Its big dark eyes looked right at them as it sat bobbing effortlessly in the water. The sea lion rolled onto its side, still eyeing them. After jerking its head as if to say "this way," the sea lion glided gracefully toward shore, making playful leaps along the way.

"C'mon," Luke said, swimming after the sea lion.

At this point, Ezzy figured 'why not' and followed. Aiden trailed after her.

The sea lion somersaulted and circled a few times, all the while heading toward shore. Soon they were very close to the rocks at the coast, but still Ezzy couldn't see any way to climb out. The sea lion circled them again and looked back as if to be sure they were watching. Then, with a flick of its flippers and tail, the sea lion shot through the water and headed straight for the rocks. Ezzy thought it might leap out like she'd seen them do in other places. But instead of jumping, the sea lion slid on its belly onto a smooth slab of rock. The ramp blended in so well with the surrounding cliff, it was impossible to see until the sea lion belly-slid onto it.

"Awesome!" Luke said. He pulled with his arms, kicked hard, and followed the sea lion, sliding onto the ramp on his stomach. Crawling further up on the rocks, he shouted back, "C'mon, Sis. It's easy."

"Guess it's my turn to play sea lion," Ezzy said before she pulled, kicked hard, and then belly-slid onto the smooth rock, trying to mimic what Luke and the sea lion had done. She didn't make it up very far and had to wiggle awkwardly the rest of the way. It wasn't very graceful, but she was out of the water. Aiden followed, mastering the belly-slide technique. Up ahead, Luke sat next to the sea lion, smiling.

They climbed to a dry rock shelf higher up on

the cliff. Passing the sea lion, Ezzy smiled and said, "Thanks, buddy."

She took off her backpack, wondering if anything inside was still dry. Luke had lost his pack somewhere along the way. She had about half a bottle of water left. She passed it around, along with a couple of energy bars her father had packed.

Luke stared toward the wide entrance of the cove. "Maybe a boat will come by soon."

"That's the plan," Ezzy said, hoping it would happen.

They peered out across the water. The sun was beginning to set, and the light grew dimmer. Ezzy's mind was racing. She wondered how late in the day boats came into the cove and what would happen if no one came. Where was the *Darwin Voyager* and what was happening onboard? And what about her dad? Was he okay? Where was he? Ezzy put her arm around Luke and sat in silence. She didn't think any of them wanted to talk about what they were thinking, what they feared.

A weird high-pitched honking sound broke the silence. Two Galápagos penguins soon slid from the ocean onto the rock ramp. The penguins hopped their way up to a little cave off to the side, which Ezzy hadn't noticed before. Once settled, the penguins honked some more and stared at the strangers curiously.

Luke suddenly jumped up. "Hey, I hear something."

"Yeah," Ezzy said. "Two really weird sounding, but cute, penguins."

"No, Sis," Luke said. "Listen."

Aiden and Ezzy got up and stood very still, listening. The penguins had stopped braying. Now, she heard it too, a faint noise growing louder. She peered through the growing darkness toward the entrance of the cove, searching and hoping for a boat.

Then Luke pointed to the sky. "Up there!"

A small white airplane was headed toward the island. They jumped up and down, yelled, and waved their arms. Ezzy pulled one of the bright green rainjackets from her backpack and waved that as well. The airplane flew past them and disappeared from view.

"Did they see us?" Luke asked.

"I don't know," Ezzy answered.

"They must be checking out the volcano," Aiden said. "We've got to do something to get their attention if they come back this way."

"Like what?" Luke asked.

That's when Ezzy remembered a few other things her father had put in the backpack that morning. She started whipping stuff out of it. First aid kit—no. Soggy toilet paper—definitely not. Soaking wet small towel—no. Her dad's Swiss Army knife—no. Where *were* they? Then she saw what she was looking for, wedged in next to a snorkeling mask. Ezzy grabbed the whistle and handed it to Luke. She took hold of one other item.

Aiden stared at what she was holding. "What's that?"

"A flare," Ezzy replied. "And my dad showed me how to use it." She hoped she remembered correctly. Ezzy pulled the top off the flare and held it over her head. Seconds later, it hissed, sparks shot out the top, and then a line of bright orange smoke rose over their heads. Caught in a breeze, the orange smoke rose higher. It was just visible in the dimming light.

They heard the airplane before they saw it. It flew back over the ridge behind them. Luke blew on the whistle as they jumped up and down, again waving and screaming at the plane. Ezzy waved the flare. As it passed, the small airplane swooped down and waggled its wings. It was so low she could see someone staring out the window.

The plane circled once, then flew back the way it had come.

"They saw us, right?" Luke questioned.

"Yeah, they definitely saw us," Ezzy answered.

"I hope they don't think we're some wonky tourists out for a hike, waving at them," Aiden said.

Ezzy looked around. "Where would we have come from? There aren't any boats here and we don't have a naturalist with us. Remember the rules. All visitors on the islands must have a naturalist with them. If nothing else, maybe they'll call someone to report us breaking the rules."

They sat on the rock shelf. It was growing dark and cool. Luke and Ezzy put on their rain jackets.

"Do you think Dad is okay?" Luke asked.

"I bet he's waiting for us in Urbina Bay," Ezzy said, trying to sound reassuring.

"Where do you think the ship is? And my family?" Aiden asked.

She shook her head. Ezzy wanted to believe that her father was safely on shore and that everyone else on the ship was still alive and okay, including Aiden's family. But she wasn't so sure. Again, they sat in silence. A little while later, Ezzy heard another noise. It didn't sound like another airplane. Luke and Aiden must have heard it too. They jumped up and stared out toward the entrance to the cove. Soon, a small white boat with a green stripe on it sped into view. It turned into the cove and headed straight for them.

Luke jumped up and down, and hugged Ezzy. "Yay!"

Aiden joined in, and Luke got squashed in a happy group hug.

Search and Rescue in Reverse

B efore they'd even gotten into the boat, Aiden, Luke, and Ezzy began telling the two park rangers onboard what had happened. An older, fit, dark-haired man held up a hand. *"Por favor,* please get in and slow down. One at a time. What are you doing here? How did you get here?"

Ezzy helped Luke into the boat and climbed in after him. Aiden followed.

"Please sir, you have to listen to us," she urged. "The *Darwin Voyager's* been hijacked. A lot of people are in danger."

"Including my family," added Aiden.

"Yeah, and my dad," said Luke. "And they took a bunch of animals."

The two park rangers looked at one another

curiously. Then the older man said, "Tell us exactly what happened."

After that, the teens explained, as quickly as they could, everything that had happened: How the *Darwin Voyager* had been taken over by poachers; how they thought John was a passenger from another ship, but he turned out to be the leader of the bad guys; and how some speedboats were going to be used to get away with the stolen animals. And then, even with Luke right there, Ezzy told them that her father thought they probably wouldn't want to leave any witnesses.

"Where's your father now?" the older man asked.

"Hopefully he jumped off the ship and swam to shore in Urbina Bay... or he's still on the ship."

The older man seemed to be in charge. He grabbed a radio from the center console of the small boat and spoke rapidly into it in Spanish. Ezzy heard him say the *Darwin Voyager* and then he turned to them. "Where is the ship headed? When did it leave?"

The teens shook their heads and Ezzy said, "We don't know. This guy John said he had some fast boats meeting them to get away on and take the animals."

The man spoke again into the radio.

Minutes later he signed off. He then turned the boat around so that they were heading out of the cove.

"Where are we going?" Ezzy asked.

"What about my dad?" Luke questioned.

"And my family?" Aiden added.

"My name is Juan Carlos," said the older man. "This is Hugo." He turned to the younger, portly ranger beside him. "We've informed the park and local authorities. They're going to call around to the ships in the area and see if anyone has seen the *Darwin Voyager*. Because of the volcanic eruption, more boats are around so hopefully someone has seen the ship."

"What about the airplane we saw?" Aiden asked. "Maybe they can go look for the ship."

Juan Carlos scanned the horizon. "It's getting dark and they cannot fly at night here."

"What about my dad?" Ezzy asked.

"Yes, of course," Juan Carlos said. "On our way to Port Villamil, we'll stop by Urbina Bay to see if he is there."

"Can't you send boats out looking for the ship?" Aiden urged. "Like the police or the navy or something?"

"This is a remote part of the islands and here in the Galápagos we have limited resources. Believe me, we'll do everything we can. I suspect we have a little bit of time. They're not going to want to make the transfer until it is completely dark, and until they are far enough away from the islands that there'll be no passing ships. The local police and, yes, even the Ecuadorian Navy are being contacted. Now you three should either sit down or hold on because I'm going to show you just how fast this boat can go. *¡Vamonos!*"

Luke sat down on the cushioned bench seat in front of the boat's center console. Aiden and Ezzy stayed standing but held tightly onto the rails along the console's sides. Juan Carlos jammed the throttles forward. The boat's twin outboard engines roared. Soon they were racing across the water.

Wind whipped Ezzy's face and the boat bounced as it flew over small waves. The speed was exhilarating, but the bouncing jolted every bone and organ in her body. She held on tight. It was getting darker, and Ezzy prayed that someone, anyone, would reach the *Darwin Voyager* in time.

They sped across the sea for what must have been about fifteen minutes before Juan Carlos made a sweeping left turn and pulled back on the throttles. As the boat slowed, Ezzy's stomach, heart, and other organs settled to their usual positions. Her eyes began to adjust to the growing darkness, and she could just make out the coast.

"We're approaching Urbina Bay. Hugo, get out the searchlight."

Hugo went to a small compartment at the bow of the boat. He unlatched the door and crawled in. A few seconds later, he returned holding what looked like a jumbo flashlight. Ezzy's eyes were better adjusted now and she could make out more of the shoreline. They were nearing the small beach at Urbina Bay.

"Okay, Hugo, light it up," Juan Carlos ordered.

Hugo pointed the big light toward the beach and

turned it on. A powerful wide beam hit the sand. Luke and Ezzy went to the bow and yelled, "Dad! Dad!"

Hugo swung the light back and forth across the beach. Nothing. Luke and Ezzy continued to shout. Juan Carlos slowed the boat further and nudged its bow onto the sand. Hugo hopped out and began searching. Ezzy headed for the bow to jump out too.

"Stay in the boat, kids," ordered Juan Carlos.

Ezzy reluctantly stayed put but kept calling out for her father.

Minutes later Hugo came back. "Sorry, there's no sign of him." He climbed back into the boat.

"Dad?" Luke whimpered.

"He must still be on the ship," Ezzy groaned.

Luke turned to her. "What if he got here, saw our note on that rock, and headed to the other cove?"

"Luke, given what we went through. I don't see how he could go there in the dark. If he swam from the ship, I think he'd be here on the beach. I bet he's still on there."

Luke's chin quivered, and she could tell tears were about to flow. Ezzy bent down and hugged him tight. "Dad's really smart. He'll find a place to hide or get away somehow." She wanted to believe it.

Hugo stashed the searchlight under the center console. Juan Carlos backed the boat up and began slowly motoring away from shore. He was about to jam the throttles forward when the radio crackled, and someone spoke in Spanish. Juan Carlos picked it up. "Juan Carlos."

After a short conversation, he signed off. "We got a report from Celebrity's ship *Flora*. They passed the *Darwin Voyager* not too long ago just south of Fernandina, heading west."

"Now what?" Aiden asked.

"We're going to Port Villamil to drop you three off and then we'll join the search team."

Ezzy thought about the map of Isabela and where they were taking them. "No! No way! That's all the way around the tip of the island. You'll lose tons of time if you go there to drop us off. This boat is way faster than the *Darwin Voyager*. Let's just go after them. We want to go with you. We have to go with you!"

"Definitely," added Aiden. "Those are our families on that ship."

"Please," Luke pleaded, giving the men his best pouty about-to-cry face.

Juan Carlos and Hugo looked at one another and shrugged. Juan Carlos turned to Hugo. "How are we doing on gas?"

"Should be good to go. I topped it off before we left."

Luke and Ezzy already had on their rain jackets. The ranger gave his jacket to Aiden. After a short radio call, he turned to the kids and announced, "Okay then, hold on!"

A Party Not to Attend

The boat rocketed across the water. Ezzy figured her body parts might do better sitting down, so she scooted in next to Luke on the bench in front of the center console. She wrapped her arm around him and snuggled in close. Aiden stayed standing. Ezzy had hoped they'd find her father at Urbina Bay, but she wasn't all that surprised he was still on the ship. She had a feeling that their buddy John planned on keeping a close eye on him.

Ezzy gave her brother a squeeze. "We'll find them," she whispered, even though, over the roar of the engines, she knew he couldn't hear her.

They passed several boats with red and green lights on their sides going in the opposite direction. Ezzy even saw another cruise ship all lit up. Then the waves got bigger and she had to hold onto the boat and Luke as they bounced, speeding across the dark sea. Aiden gripped the rail tightly, bending his legs to absorb each bounce. When they hit an even larger wave, the entire boat went airborne and then landed with a pounding jolt. Aiden nearly fell and Luke almost flew off the seat. Ezzy held onto him tight. Juan Carlos slowed the boat.

Ezzy turned to him. "Where are we?"

"We've just rounded the southern tip of Fernandina." He pointed to their right. In the distance, against a backdrop of brightening stars, she could see a towering silhouette; it was the dark upside-down soup bowl shape of the island.

Juan Carlos pulled back on the throttles some more and picked up the radio. He made a quick call and then turned to the teens. "The Ecuadorian Navy has a ship to the south of here patrolling for illegal fishermen and shark finners. It's changing course and heading up this way. We've also got several police and park boats coming. Based on the report from *Flora's* captain, my guess is the *Darwin Voyager* is not too much farther ahead. Probably north of here and to the west."

"Let's go!" urged Aiden.

"*Lo siento,*" said Juan Carlos. "Sorry, I was told to wait here for reinforcements."

"What?" Ezzy blurted out. "But we can't wait. If they get off the boat before anyone gets there, who knows what they'll do. They might sink the ship or something."

"I have my orders."

Luke stared at Juan Carlos teary-eyed. "It's my dad."

"Please, sir," Ezzy pleaded. "Can't we at least go closer to see if they're okay?"

Juan Carlos sighed. "I guess we could try to get the ship in sight."

They began motoring slowly through the waves. Ezzy kept her eyes peeled ahead, looking for any sign of the *Darwin Voyager*. Aiden went to the bow and stared out over the water. Luke had a tight hold of Ezzy's hand. She gave it a squeeze.

They cruised for what seemed a long time. The only sound was the puttering of the engines. Everyone was silent as they each concentrated on looking for the *Darwin Voyager*. Then Hugo pointed off to the left and ahead. "There!"

Ezzy squinted, trying to see what he was pointing to.

"The ship's dark, but there are some lights moving around at the stern."

Once she knew what to look for, Ezzy could see it too. "Maybe they're unloading the animals."

Juan Carlos slowed the boat further, and they cruised quietly closer. Soon they could hear someone barking orders. The boat glided to a stop. Ezzy turned to Juan Carlos and whispered, "Why are we stopping? They're right there."

Juan Carlos put a finger to his lips. He made a quiet call on the radio, giving the latitude and longitude of their position. He then whispered, "It's too dangerous, Señorita."

"But what about all the people onboard?"

"We need to wait for the *policía*. But, *mis amigos*, you three made all the difference by finding your way across that island and letting us know what was going on."

"But... "

A spotlight on the ship suddenly came on and began rotating across the sea. It was headed their way. "They must have seen us on radar," swore Hugo.

"Hold on kids," Juan Carlos urged, swinging the boat around. He was about to push the throttle forward when the spotlight hit them. A voice barked loudly across the water, "Don't move your vessel!"

Juan Carlos's hand was still on the throttle, readying to shove it forward.

"I'm serious," shouted the man on the ship. "If you take off now, people will get hurt. My boats are much faster than yours."

Juan Carlos stepped back, lowering his hand. Ezzy slumped in her seat. Luke put his head in his hands and Aiden stood staring angrily at the ship ahead.

"Don't worry kids, help is on the way," Juan Carlos told them.

"Yeah, but how soon will they get here?" Aiden groaned.

A boat approached, entering the spotlight's beam. The light revealed a stack of cages in the back. The rangers gasped when they saw the animals trapped inside. Two men stood at the bow of the boat with their guns trained on the park vessel. The guns weren't of the dart variety. It was goatee goon and his stringy haired mustached buddy. "Okay, nice and slow now, motor over to the ship."

Juan Carlos grimaced and slowly brought their boat around. Soon they were pulling up beside another speedboat, behind the *Darwin Voyager*. Flashlights shone on their faces.

"You again." It was John. "And I thought I was finally rid of you, lost for good or, even better, sacrificed to the volcano. Well, I guess you've come to join the party. Please disembark and watch your step. Wouldn't want you three little darlings to get hurt."

He laughed, and it made Ezzy's insides roil. No wicked witch needed here, they had their own well-tailored version—an insane dude in a polo shirt and heavily starched, wrinkle-free khakis. John's men watched attentively as they climbed out of the park boat and onto the *Darwin Voyager's* stern platform.

"Please follow my men," John said. "And no one will get hurt."

"I've heard that before," Aiden muttered.

"Where's my dad?" Luke asked.

"Oh, you'll be joining him soon, Master Luke, no worries."

"They know all about you and your plans," Ezzy announced.

"No worries, Miss Ezzy. Now be a good little girl and do what you're told, for once. Besides, as I told you, the world will thank me for saving all of these precious species. I'm really the hero here."

Ezzy hissed at the man, wishing she could do more.

They were marched up a deck and then forward through the lounge. No one was around.

"Down the stairs," ordered goatee goon.

With the two rangers at the back, they went down a deck.

"Next deck down, keep going!"

Ezzy wondered where the gunmen were taking them. When she saw the large metal hatchway ahead, she had a pretty good idea—and it wasn't good. They still hadn't seen any of the crew or other passengers. Then she heard muffled voices.

"I've got a few more for you," said one of the men from behind.

Another fake officer stood at the entrance to the engine room. "Right this way."

As soon as Ezzy entered the room, she saw the others. The ship's remaining officers, crew, and all the passengers were tied up, gagged, and spread out across the deck. She immediately searched for her father. Luke saw him first and ran over. He was sitting with his back against a wall next to Grandpa and Grandma Jones. Ezzy heard her dad yell their names through his gag. She ran to him as well. Aiden found his family.

"How sweet. A little family reunion," said the stringy haired man who'd just entered the room and was once again lovingly stroking his mustache. "And two new guests as well."

Juan Carlos and Hugo looked ready to explode.

"Don't even think of playing heroes," he told them. "Okay, everyone have a seat and get comfy." He pointed to another man in the engine room. "Tie up and gag our new guests. It's about time for us to leave this little get-together."

The guards used plastic zip ties to bind the new prisoners' wrists and legs. Then they used restaurant napkins as gags.

"Now you all enjoy the rest of the cruise, though, due to unforeseen circumstances, it's going to be shorter than planned," stringy hair said, snickering. "Besides, accidents happen in remote places like the Galápagos. Poorly maintained engines on a ship can cause terrible, dangerous, even explosive problems."

The man checked his watch and went to the side of one of the ship's engines. He appeared to be fiddling with something. Afterward, he turned to the group and saluted. "See ya."

As soon as the last of John's men left, it went dark. The only light in the room came from a faint red luminescence. The glow came from where the stringy haired dude had been just before leaving. Ezzy hoped she was wrong about what was there and what was creating the red glow. But in her heart, she knew—it was a bomb. They weren't going to just sink the ship; they were going to blow it to pieces, along with all of the potential witnesses.

Ezzy could hear people moving around and trying to break their bonds. A few passengers sobbed. Her father was fidgeting next to her. Ezzy figured he was trying to get free of the ties binding his wrists and ankles.

Ezzy tried to break free as well, but it was no use. The ties were too tight and too sturdy. She was scared, but also angrier than she'd ever been in her life. She'd already crawled through giant tortoise turds, outrun a river of lava, and even jumped into shark-infested waters. *And now a bomb?* Ezzy wondered how much time they had left. Could this really be the end of the new, adventurous, brave Ezzy? She felt like she was just getting started. Then she thought of her dad and Luke. She turned to her father and through her gag tried to say, "I love you, Dad and I'm sorry for being so sarcastic and all the bad things I've ever done."

They shuffled closer. Then Ezzy heard muffled talking nearby and bodies moving. It was Grandpa and Grandma Jones. She figured they were probably panicking, saying their goodbyes, or maybe he was having that heart attack she had worried about while they were hiking. Then, very unexpectedly, she heard

Grandma Jones clearly say, "Phil, do you have your knife?"

"It was in my sock. But they found it when they tied me up."

"Oh, cracklins!"

Ezzy didn't know what cracklins were or what they had to do with anything, but she shouted through the gag, "There's a knife in my backpack." She figured it came out as a muffled unintelligible grunt, but she tried again anyway, "There's a knife in my backpack!" She'd slung the backpack over one shoulder before getting out of the boat and no one had noticed. Or the bad guys just figured she had water and sunscreen in it. She felt someone nudge her. Using her teeth, Grandma Jones pulled off Ezzy's gag. "What did you say?"

"My dad's Swiss Army knife and a flashlight are in my backpack."

"Good girl!"

With some artful twisting of limbs and teamwork, the older couple opened Ezzy's backpack, dumped its contents onto the deck and felt around for the Swiss Army knife and the flashlight.

"Here's the light," Grandma Jones said, switching it on and turning it to shine on the area where they'd dumped out the backpack. Grandpa Jones immediately shuffled over to where the Swiss Army knife lay and rolled over onto it. After a few seconds of grappling with the blade, he sat up. His hands were free, and he quickly cut away the ties at his ankles. Soon Grandma

Jones was free as well. She cut Ezzy loose and gave her a quick hug. "With that knife, you may have just saved us all."

Even though they were still in grave danger, Ezzy nodded with pride. The two of them began ungagging and freeing the others as fast as they could. Meanwhile Grandpa Jones went to look at the bomb. "Okay everyone, we have fifteen minutes before this place goes boom. Where's the captain?"

One of the officers who'd been freed spoke up, "They took him off the ship."

"Folks, me and the missus here are ex-military. And I'm happy to tell you we met during explosives training."

"Whoa," Ezzy heard Luke mutter.

"Officers, if you would, go up and get ready to abandon ship. We'll try to defuse the bomb, but no guarantees."

"On it," said two of the officers as they rushed out.

"Do you need any help?" asked Dr. Skylar.

"Yes," replied Grandma Jones. "I need you to get yourself, your kids, and the rest of these people out of here."

Once everyone was free of their ties, the Skylars led the way out of the engine room and up through the ship. All the lights suddenly came on. It was so bright, Ezzy had to squint at first. She tried to remember where they were supposed to go to abandon ship.

They'd done an emergency drill the first day. Luckily her dad had paid better attention. "This way, everyone, up to deck four mid-ship!"

Seven short blasts of the ship's horn and one long blast rang out. An officer came on the intercom. "This is definitely not a drill. Abandon ship!"

They didn't have time to get their lifejackets from their cabins, so they went straight to their emergency stations. The crew began to prepare the lifeboats, which sat ready to be raised off their cradles and then lowered to the sea. Several life rafts were thrown overboard. Ezzy heard them inflate when they hit the water. She stood hugging and comforting Luke, while her father did what he could to help what was left of the crew.

As people started boarding the lifeboats, Ezzy wondered how much time was left before the bomb went kaboom—ten minutes maybe. Dr. Skylar tried to get her and Luke into the lifeboats while he helped others, but they wouldn't leave his side. Aiden climbed in with his family, including his two sisters who were cellphone-free and maybe, for the first-time on the trip, uninterested in taking selfies. Finally, when nearly all the other passengers were aboard, Ezzy, Luke and their father climbed into the lifeboat. There was still no sign of the Joneses. Ezzy figured they must still be trying to defuse the bomb. She made a mental note that if she was still alive after the next few minutes, she would thank them profusely and find out their real names.

"Deploy the lifeboats!" shouted an officer.

"No!" yelled Phil, also known as Grandpa Jones, as he ran up on deck. Seconds later he wound up and threw something, hard as he could, off the ship. It flew into the darkness and landed with a faint splash. Everyone sat in stunned silence. Seconds later, a deep boom echoed through the sea and water gushed upward. The bomb had exploded under water.

Phil hugged his wife, who had joined him. They were both breathing hard. "Once I figured out there were no booby traps on the thing, we just pulled it off and ran!"

Everyone cheered and clapped. People began getting out of the lifeboats and hugging their family or the nearest person. Guests, officers, park rangers, naturalists, and crew all hugged one another.

Dr. Skylar knelt down and wrapped Luke and Ezzy in his arms. "Thank god. I was so worried about you two."

"We were worried about you, too," Luke said, and his dad laughed.

"Thanks for all the stuff you put in the backpack," Ezzy added. "It saved us."

"So, tell me everything. What happened?"

While they explained what happened on the island and how the park rangers found them, the ship's crew quickly got back to work. The officers and park rangers went to the bridge to contact the authorities.

"You two are amazing," their father said. "I'm so proud of you. Your mother would have been proud, too. I knew you could do it, Ezzy."

Ezzy smiled. She was proud of everything she'd done that day. She felt better about herself than she had in a very long time. Maybe she was a lot more like her mother than she'd thought.

"Aiden was pretty amazing too," Ezzy said, looking around for him. He was standing with his family not too far away. She waved him over. Aiden said something to his parents and then joined them.

"Thanks Aiden," Dr. Skylar said, shaking his hand. "For all you did out there on the island."

"Yeah, thanks," Ezzy added.

"No problem. Piece of cake."

Luke wrapped himself around Aiden's legs. "Yeah, and thanks for the piggyback rides."

"Anytime, sport."

Ezzy wanted to hug Aiden too, but suddenly she felt overwhelmingly awkward. Instead she asked, "How's your leg?"

"It's fine, especially given the nurse I had to clean it."

She felt her face flush.

"Let me take a look at that, son," her father said. "You two as well. It looks like we've got some major cleaning up to do and a bunch of cuts to take care of. Guess all's well that ends pretty good."

Aiden stared at the man like he was a little daffy. Luke and Ezzy laughed. "All's well that ends *well*, Dad," Luke said. "But what about the kidnapped animals?"

"I'm sure the authorities will track down John and his gang," his father replied. "Let's get you cleaned up. You must be exhausted and hungry."

The minute he said it, Ezzy realized she was ready to drop and super starved. She'd even go for some raw fish. *Okay, well maybe not that hungry.* She waved to Aiden as he went back to his family and they headed down to their cabins. On the way, her father asked one of the crew members if they could get a seriously large late-night snack.

Survival of the Fittest

The next morning Ezzy slept in. It was pure heaven. She probably would have stayed in bed longer if her stomach weren't growling like an angry bear after months in hibernation. She got up, dressed, and knocked on her father and Luke's cabin. No answer. They were probably already at breakfast.

The dining room was packed and extremely noisy. Everyone was talking to one another and laughing, including the remaining real crew and officers. Ezzy figured having a shared near-death experience would do that. She made her way to where Luke and her father were sitting. They were at a table with Aiden and his family, along with Grandpa and Grandma Jones. When they saw her coming, they squeezed in another chair and place-setting.

"There she is," her father said. "We thought you might sleep right through the day."

"Probably would've if I wasn't so starved."

Her dad turned to the elderly couple that had saved the ship. "We're quite honored to sit with our very own heroes, Phil and Gracie Smith."

Really? Their name is Smith, Ezzy thought. *That's almost as generic as Jones.* She snickered to herself and said, "You were amazing last night. Thanks to you we're not all fish food."

Gracie Smith laughed. "Honey, you weren't so bad yourself. And we had no intention of becoming fish food. We just wished we could have stopped the whole thing sooner. Once we realized what was going on, we looked for an opportunity to do something, but it was too risky. We didn't want to endanger anyone else."

"Are you really ex-military?" Ezzy asked. "I just thought you were old people."

"Ezzy!" her father said.

"That's okay," Phil said laughing. "One, we are old people, and it happens to all of us. And two, we do like to ham up the elderly thing and then surprise people by being quicker and more with it than they think." He winked at his wife and gave her a kiss.

"And yes," Gracie said. "We are ex-military, but sweetie, I can't tell you exactly which branch we were in." She winked.

"CIA?" Aiden asked. "Special Forces?"

The Smiths just smiled.

"No matter," Dr. Skylar said. "We're all so thankful you were there."

"And I heard you three rascals had quite the adventure on the island," Phil said to Ezzy.

"Yup, an adventure all right." Ezzy nodded to Aiden and ruffled Luke's hair.

Just then Geovana and Jorge came by the table. They each hugged the Smiths and said thank you. Then they turned to Luke, Aiden, and Ezzy. "As for you three, you do know that you are not supposed to be on any island without a naturalist," Geovana scolded.

"And you broke nearly all the rules about staying on the trails and disrupting the flora and fauna," Jorge added.

"But..." Ezzy stuttered.

The naturalists broke into smiles. "Just kidding!" laughed Geovana. "You did great, and we'd love to hear exactly how you made your way from Urbina Bay to Tagus Cove."

"Thanks for the arrow," Luke said.

Geovana bowed. "My pleasure. Now we've got to get to work and plan for this afternoon's excursion." She looked at Luke. "Lots of animals."

"Oh great," Ezzy said sarcastically.

Luke turned to her. "Sis, c'mon. The animals are cool. Look how much they helped us on the island."

"Yeah, yeah," she said. "I think I can handle it. Except for snakes and maybe sharks, and maybe those booger-sneezing iguanas, and definitely no more tortoise turds, and..."

Luke giggled and put his hand over her mouth. "It'll be awesome."

She nodded and hugged him. "Just kidding. The animals are cool. Well, at least most of them. As long as I'm with you and Dad it will be awesome."

They finished breakfast and went up to the stern deck. Overnight, the ship had cruised to Port Villamil and anchored just offshore. As they watched, two speedboats driven by men in official looking jumpsuits cruised into view, heading toward shore. Following behind was a big gray Ecuadorian Navy ship. The ship passed close by and gave a blast of its horn. The captain from the *Darwin Voyager* along with the other kidnapped crew were onboard and waved before pointing to the back deck. It was loaded with crates and cages filled with animals. Sitting alongside them was a group of men with their hands tied behind their backs.

"Woohoo!" Luke jumped up and down and waved at them.

"Yeah!" Ezzy said, "They got 'em." She stared hard in search of John and thought she saw him tied up along with the other men. Even though he probably couldn't hear her, she shouted, "Guess Darwin was right. Survival of the fittest!"

Her father added, "Crime doesn't play."

"Pay, Dad," Luke said. "It's crime doesn't pay."

"That too," he said, grabbing Luke and Ezzy. "I love you guys. Hey, we've got some time this morning, while they get things straightened out on the ship. What do you want to do?"

Luke shrugged.

"I think I'll go read that book you gave me on Darwin," Ezzy said. "Seems sort of appropriate."

Her father laughed.

She looked at him and asked, "This was number one on mom's wonder list, right?"

He nodded.

"Honestly Dad, I'm not sure I want to know what number two is."

"You're gonna love it!"

Note from the Author:
Real vs Made Up

As a scientist, I've been incredibly fortunate to go repeatedly to the Galápagos Islands for research and as an advisor to Celebrity Cruises' small expedition ships. Going to the Galápagos is always exciting and wondrous, and you never know what you might see in terms of wildlife and behavior. Much of this book is based on real science and things that have really happened in the Galápagos, but there is also a component of make-believe. Can you guess which of the following is real and which is made up? (answers start on page 199)

Animals perform their courtship rituals close to the hiking trails.

Someone once tried to smuggle iguanas out of the Galápagos and was caught when their luggage started moving.

There are giant tortoise tunnels from the lowlands up to the highlands.

A hawk dropped a snake on a visiting hiker.

A woman fell onto a carpet of marine iguanas when her walking stick broke.

Land iguanas cut trails through the brush and rocky slopes.

You can walk through old lava tubes.

Marine iguanas sneeze salt.

A volcanic eruption occurred unexpectedly on Wolf Volcano.

There is a coral reef at Urbina Bay that was raised above the sea in an earthquake and it now resembles a forest of giant rock mushrooms.

You can hike from Urbina Bay to Tagus Cove.

Many of the Galápagos animals are endemic (unique to the Islands).

If a volcano is erupting, you should run toward it.

Animals perform their courtship rituals close to the hiking trails.

Real. Because the islands and animals are well protected by the rules of the Galápagos National Park, which are enforced by rangers and the licensed naturalists, the animals co-exist in peace with humans and are unafraid.

Someone once tried to smuggle iguanas out of the Galápagos and was caught when their luggage started moving.

Real!

There are giant tortoise tunnels from the lowlands up to the highlands.

Made-up! Tortoise trails are visible from some of the hiking paths, but the tortoises do not use tunnels to travel to and from the highlands. Though some giant tortoises do spend the hot/wet season eating vegetation in the lowlands and then migrate to the highlands in the cooler/drier season.

A hawk dropped a snake on a visiting hiker.

Real, or at least I heard this story from a naturalist leading a hike.

A woman fell onto a carpet of marine iguanas when her walking stick broke.

Real, this happened during a hike I was on, on the island of Fernandina where there are literally thousands of marine iguanas.

Land iguanas cut trails through the brush and rocky slopes.

Made-up. Where it is sandy, land iguanas leave evidence of their travels with trails made by their tails, but they scamper easily through the brush.

You can walk through old lava tubes.

Real. On the island of Santa Cruz there are ancient lava tubes that are large enough to walk through.

Marine iguanas sneeze salt.

Real. Marine iguanas dive into the ocean and feed on algæ. To rid themselves of excess salt they sneeze it out their noses.

A volcanic eruption occurred unexpectedly on Wolf Volcano.

Real. In May 2015, Wolf Volcano on Isabela Island erupted unexpectedly. People expected the next eruption to occur on Fernandina or one of the other volcanoes on

Isabela. Celebrity's ship *Xpedition* veered from its normal cruise track and was the first on site. Just after midnight, the guests aboard got a spectacular view of the fiery lava fountains.

There is a coral reef at Urbina Bay that was raised above the sea in an earthquake and it now resembles a forest of giant rock mushrooms.

Real! In an earthquake in 1954 the coast of Isabela was uplifted and the land rose about fifteen feet. A coral reef was raised out of the water. Fishermen first discovered it by the smell of dead fish!

You can hike from Urbina Bay to Tagus Cove.

Made-up. It is a lot farther than depicted in the story and it would be extremely difficult and wild terrain to pass through. In addition, it would be against park rules!

Many of the Galápagos animals are endemic (unique to the Islands).

Real! Because of their remote location and the conditions, many animals that live in the Galápagos have evolved over time to become unique species.

If a volcano is erupting, you should run toward it.

Made-up. Volcanic eruptions can be viewed from a safe distance away, but it is always important to get information from local authorities as to what a safe distance is and where to go.

Also real are:

Mockingbirds on Española will come close looking for water. One landed on my head once.

There is a unique species of pink iguanas found only on Wolf Volcano on the island of Isabela.

Pencil urchin spines contribute to sand on some of the islands and children in the Galápagos used to use them like chalk.

Iguanas have been caught over the blowhole and were seen to "fly".

There are giant grasshoppers (locusts) that jump when startled on the trails.

The cormorants in the Galápagos are the world's only flightless cormorants.

Lava cactus are called pioneer plants because they are one of the first things to start growing on hardened lava flows.

We once reported seeing a submerged red light that was an illegal fishing net.

And, I love the Galápagos. Very REAL!

Acknowledgments

My sincerest gratitude goes to all those who have encouraged and supported me, and made me laugh when things get tough. We all need positive people in our lives. Take a minute to say something nice or encouraging to someone you love, like, or even a complete stranger. You never know how much it might help.

Special thanks to all the people I have worked with in the Galápagos Islands and who continue to make it one of the most wondrous places in the world. I especially want to thank the Ecuadorian government, Galápagos National Park Directorate, rangers, naturalists, companies, and visitors who together provide the economic incentive and conservation needed to protect these amazing islands and their wild inhabitants. Thank you to Celebrity Cruises for their continued commitment to protecting the Galápagos, minimizing their environmental impact, and ensuring that their guests follow park rules and get the very best experience possible. The Galápagos Islands truly showcase how humans and wildlife can co-exist in a way that respects and protects Nature. All of the characters in the book are a work of fiction, though a few people may recognize some of the names in the story.

Thank you to all of the folks at Tumblehome for their hard work and input, commitment to education and learning, and especially to Yu-Yi Ling and to publisher Penny Noyce for her enthusiasm, excellent editing skills and thoughtful comments, which greatly improved the text. And a note of thanks to her son, Owen Liu, who introduced us. Thanks to illustrator Melissa Logies for her wonderful and speedily accomplished cover.

Huge gratitude goes to my test readers and their parents: Hugo and Grandma Kathy; Andrew and Andrea; the entire Tougas family; and Carlos and July! Your amazing comments and notes are incredibly helpful and inspire me to keep the fun adventures coming!

And finally, a very big virtual hug for my family and friends who laugh at my jokes and keep me sane. Special thanks to Dave and his family who've brought a whole new level of joy, laughter, and love into my life.

About The Author

Dr. Ellen Prager is a marine scientist and author, widely recognized for her expertise and ability to make science entertaining and understandable for people of all ages. She currently works as a freelance writer, consultant, and science advisor to Celebrity Cruises in the Galápagos Islands. She was previously the Chief Scientist for the Aquarius Reef Base program in Key Largo, Florida and the Assistant Dean at the University of Miami's Rosenstiel School of Marine and Atmospheric Science. Dr. Prager has built a national reputation as a scientist and spokesperson, serving as a consultant for the Disney movie *Moana* and appearing on The Today Show, Good Morning America, CBS Early Show, Larry King, CNN, Fox News, The Weather Channel, and Discovery Channel. She is the author of the successful *Tristan Hunt and the Sea Guardians* series of middle-grade adventure novels.